Elsa

CW00602235

The New Moon with the Old Moon in her Arms

By the same author

Novels

The Borrower
Green Lights Are Blue
Sounds of a Drunken Summer
Encores for a Dilettante
The Prison Architect(s)
That which is bright rises twice
The Autobiography of Cassandra, Princess and Prophetess of Troy
Positions with White Roses
Remnants of an Unknown Woman

Fictionalised History

A Full Moon of Women: 29 Word Portraits of Notable Women from Different Times and Places

Short Story Collections

Bastards: Footnotes to History
Nightschool for Saints
Top Stories No 16
Needlepoint
13

Poetry Collections

Mirrors for Small Beasts
Unmuzzled Ox Encyclopedia

Plays

The Abstract Wife
One Must Be Two
Breakfast Past Noon

The New Moon
with the
Old Moon in
her Arms

A true story assembled from scholarly hearsay

Ursule Molinaro

The Women's Press

First published by The Women's Press Ltd 1990
A member of the Namara Group
34 Great Sutton Street, London EC1V 0DX

Copyright © Ursule Molinaro, 1990

British Library Cataloguing in Publication Data
Molinaro, Ursule
The new moon with the old moon in her arms.
I. Title
813'.54 [F]

ISBN 0-7043-5057-2

Phototypeset by Input Typesetting Ltd, London
Printed and bound in Great Britain by
BPCC Hazell Books, Aylesbury, Bucks, England
Member of BPCC Ltd.

For BJG
who scoured many libraries
& transported many weighty volumes
that laid the groundwork for this book.

& for Mopsus
who lay by me throughout.

Late, late yestreen I saw the new moone wi'
the auld moone in hir arme.

Sir Patrick Spens (Spence), Minstrelsy of the
Scottish Border

Someone threw a stone at me this morning.

Prematurely, & therefore unlawfully. No one may hurt a Thargelia volunteer, not even with words, until the 6th of Thargelion, Expulsion Day, which is still one whole moon away. For 29 more days I'm inviolate. As sacred as public property. Richly fed & housed at city expense.

Which was not what prompted me, 325 nights ago, to get up in the middle of dinner at my parents' house
—Where I was being fed not richly, but adequately: My mother values economy in the selection of her cooking slaves. Homeliness for the females, whose foreheads she deliberately disfigures when she brands them. —
& walk out into a grainy full-moon night. To go knocking on the door of a city father interrupting his dinner & volunteer my normal, healthy, 30-year-old body to be stoned to death on next year's Expulsion Day.

After watching the stoning to death of 2 crooked creatures earlier that afternoon 325½ days ago during last year's Thargelia.

In which I took an active part. Surprising myself & others with the accuracy of my aim.

Which became the subject of that evening's dinner conversation between my parents. Who consider themselves too modern to participate in what my father calls: antiquated superstitious mummeries kept alive to appease the populace. My parents were voicing their disapproval of my active participation, of which an also participating slave had promptly informed them. Which prompted my father to remark that: I was behaving like one of the slaves.

Which both my parents have taken turns remarking

every year except one, the one year I did not participate:
the summer of my 12th year, when I was trying to please
my father during dinner, on the evenings of Expulsion
Days. Which both my parents make a point of spending
barricaded in their house.

Where I was still living. Not richly, but adequately. An
embarrassment, especially to my father: his only child a
daughter. Unmarried still, at 30 & childless. A stone-
throwing poetess without an audience, unable to earn her
living with her craft.

Which was not what prompted me either. At least not
directly. But the voice of the moon goddess Circe, urging
inside my head: That I sacrifice my normal, healthy,
intelligent, better-than-average-looking/thinking self to
save the moon's place in the sky.
    Convincing me that the fate of the moon was directly
linked to the cause of women, for which I had thrown my
stone earlier that afternoon. Hoping to throw out the
growing prejudice against professional women in general,
& against writing women in particular. Poetesses who can
no longer find an audience, not even among women.
    I had the strange sensation that another, more lucid
consciousness was slowly taking over my body.
    Which rose from the stone seat on which it had sat,
eating dinner. & floated through the rooms of the house,
past slaves who interrupted their work to watch it float
past.
    Past the over-lifesize stone porter with which my father
had replaced the live slave who used to guard the entrance,
but had grown weak & embarrassing looking. Who eventually died, crouched behind his stone successor.

& out into the moon-lit streets. Along which it walked, determined & unafraid.

Confident that it would not feel the ordeal of its sacrifice, because it was inhabited by the immortal moon goddess Circe, who knew how to kill pain with the magic of herbs.

PREMISE

I: The seed of global destruction, currently feared in the form of a nuclear blow-up, was planted during the 4th millennium BC, at the beginning of the Taurean age (4000 to 2000 BC, approximately —each age is assumed to last 2,160 years; a complete circuit is assumed to last 25,290 years—)
when militarism abruptly replaced egalitarianism.

Militarism & hierarchy are vertical-masculine-concepts, symbolized by erection/structure. Egalitarianism is a horizontal-female-concept, symbolized by water. Which flows on & nowhere piles up, always seeking its own level.

The beginning Taurean age had introduced the cultivation of the soil (Taurus: fixed earth; female) & with it a fixed way of life which gradually replaced the (Gemini: mutable air; androgynous) mobility of hunting & gathering.
As illustrated by the interplay of yin & yang in the hexagrams of the *I-Ching*, the Chinese *Book of Changes*, the doubling of either produces its opposite. Accordingly, agriculture, with its female-earth emphasis, abruptly produced (male-oriented) militarism during the female-earth age, when it gave birth to the notion of ownership.
—Possession, the bane of the human race.— Which

extended from the ownership of land to the owning of
other beings. First animal, then human. To slavery, & the
domestication of women.
& gave birth to the notion of legitimacy, including the
legitimacy/illegitimacy of children & their mothers.
(Gradually excluding women from making vital decisions,
even about their own bodies.) & led in a straight line to
militarism, to defend the legitimately owned land. Cattle.
Chattel.

The first split of the atom occurred 5 millennia before Lise
Meitner

—the Austrian physicist & mathematician, whose research
in atomic physics & work with uranium fission was as
pivotal to civilization as the first use of fire—

when the female participation in the creative process began
to be belittled, if not condemned. When fecundation &
incubation took on value distinctions that equated them
with: mind over matter. Or: master & slave. Equating
women with a furrow into which man sowed his seed.
When the new solar theologies began belittling the moon,
without whose nurturing balance the seed of life cannot
withstand the sun.

II: Since to know the seed is divine, in the two-fold
meaning of godly & prophetic, the moon goddess Circe
read the social demotion of women as a threat to the
maintenance of the universe, which relies on the balance
between the male & female poles of life. & she began to
fear for the moon's place in the sky.

After 3 millennia of deliberation & dwindling believers
she decides, on Thargelion 6, 294 BC, to travel to Athens,

one of the cradles of steadily increasing male domination, & participate in that city's yearly expulsion rite, which takes place on that date, in an attempt to throw out the calamitous condition of women that makes her fear for the moon's place in the sky.

Standing invisible in the chanting, stone-throwing crowd, the moon goddess Circe borrows the right arm & hand (normally used for writing poems) of a 30-year-old Athenian poetess unmarried, childless, & without an audience to throw a white marble ball, the size of a distant full moon, or child's head, at the sacrificial groom. Hitting him in the temple.

Later that same evening, during dinner, she fills the poetess' mind with the impulse to volunteer as an untraditionally attractive fig-tree bride for the following Thargelia (Thargelion 6, 293 BC), in case the well-aimed marble ball was not enough to expel the current predominance of mortal men.

Convincing the poetess that the conscious self-sacrifice of an intelligent, beautiful woman in her prime★ will prove more effective than the best of best-aimed stones in putting an end to the calamitous condition of women in general, & of poetesses in Athens in particular. That her sacrifice will restore the balance between the 2 poles of life.

★The poetess later points out to the moon goddess Circe who has, by then, taken up residence inside the poetess' body, that: being 30 years old in Athens is the beginning of a calamitous condition for women. Who are considered too old to be marriageable, & are usually not old enough to be wealthily widowed.

There no longer is a prime age for women in Athens: the poetess informs the moon goddess Circe: because their hopes of becoming wealthy (widows) are being shattered by a recent legislation which aims at restricting the right of women to own land, cattle, or slaves.

Which will restore the balance of the universe.
Which will restore the good housekeeping of earlier, pre-
militaristic, pre-hierarchical, pre-agricultural millennia.
Which will assure the moon's place in the sky.
Further convincing the poetess that her shapely body will
barely feel the stones. Whose impact will be numbed, if
not annulled, by the ecstasy-inducing worthiness of her
cause. & by chewing laurel leaves. Which are the exclusive
prerogative of Pythian priestesses, but which Circe prom-
ises to supply in unlimited quantities if the poetess accepts.

Mounichion 7

    28 more days, & I will have lived out my 1-year lifespan
as a Thargelia bride.

    On the morning of Expulsion Day, Thargelion 6, my
attendant will wake me if I have slept, during the last
night of my life. He will bathe me in softened water, &
rub a special pain-numbing lotion into my skin. I will
drink a special pain-numbing potion, while he dresses my
30-year-old body as though for a wedding, adorning it with
a necklace of pale white figs.

    —Which will feel cool & moist like a lover's hand
against my sun- or perhaps fear-flushed neck. —

    Regally I will walk down the 14 municipal steps. Toward
my partner. Who will be wearing a necklace of black figs.
& may or may not offer to take my hand, to steady me or
himself as we slowly walk side by side through sun-
drenched crowded city streets. Absorbing the sins &
illnesses, calamities & fears of our fellow citizens. Preceded
by flutists who play the fig-branch melody. Past hedges of
Athenians adults & craning children holding:

stones
& budding willow branches
& red-flowered stems of sea onion —(Only the lawless onion sprouts in the wane & withers in the waxing of the moon.)—
with which they will strike us 7 times gently across our sex organs. To stimulate our fertility during the symbolic mating of 2 fig trees, which we will enact outside the city gates.

Where we have been driven by the pressure of bodies following more & more closely behind us of arms that have begun to aim the hoarded stones of mouths—with bared teeth—chanting: OUT WITH FAMINE, IN WITH HEALTH & WEALTH.

Which becomes a single-voiced roar which engulfs our dazed dying bodies like an ocean.

IMPULSION & EXPULSION are the 2 primary principles behind most religious rites. A breathing in of hope, a breathing out of fear. & since fear is more ubiquitous than hope, expulsion rites predominate:
A victim is selected or self-impelled to bear the sins & burdens of the collective away with him or her into death.

(The custom of the Sin Eater —persons who professionally attend funerals & symbolically eat the deceaseds' sins in the form of food & drink laid out for them near the corpse or the coffin— still exists in Appalachia.)

During earliest times the sacrificed body was eaten by all —except for certain choice pieces set aside for goddesses or gods (the entrails for lunar deities; the heart for later

gods of the sun)— in the belief that the eaters ingested
the hard-earned purity & sublimation of the martyred
flesh, which saved them from a fate similar to the one they
had just witnessed. Or inflicted.
Later, the officiating priestesses or priests ate the flesh &
drank the blood in the name of the collective.
& still later, the sacrificed body was again —it still is—
  eaten by the whole congregation, in the symbolic form of
bread & wine.

During the expulsion rite known as the THARGELIA which
took place in Athens on the 6th day of the 11th month of
the Athenian (lunar) calendar

(Thargelion, a 'full' month of 30 days, approximately from
April 27 to May 26, during a 'regular' year, which had 354
days)

2 allegedly drugged human beings were slowly paraded
through the streets of the city, wearing strings of figs
around their necks. They were *pharmakoi*, (same root as:
pharmacy), living cleansers or purifiers, designated to
absorb the sins, illnesses, fears & calamities of their fellow
citizens, & carry them away outside the city gates.
Where they enacted the mating ritual of 2 fig trees which
was sometimes acted out realistically before at least 1 of
them was stoned to death by the crowd.
The fig the tree as well as the fruit was a purger, &
warded off evil.
The stones killed from a distance, & covered the victim's
sin-soaked corpse, protecting onlookers from contami-
nation, & reabsorption of the thrown-away sins, ills, etc.,
for the 24 hours the body was left to lie where it had fallen.
After that period all evil was thought to have safely

disappeared, & the corpse was burned on the wood of wild, non-fruitbearing trees.

The second victim was sometimes allowed to escape. Which was also the custom for sacrificial animals. Usually goats; hence the term: (e)scape goat.

Initially, *pharmakoi* were respected magicians, empowered to heal or to poison, who performed the purification rites themselves. Taking their own lives at the end, or merely leaving the purified city & going into exile. Which was considered a great hardship by Athenians who didn't think life outside their city was worth living.

But by the end of the 6th century BC, the continued spectacle of their victimization had reduced the *pharmakoi* to objects of ridicule & comic abuse. A grotesque, often deformed couple, decked out in wedding regalia —one of them the transvestite caricature of a bride, reserved for the sins, fears, illnesses & calamities of the women— that went through coupling motions in the hailstorm of stones thrown at them by the watching crowd.

They were recruited from among deficient slaves —with branded foreheads— offered by their masters. Or they were volunteers, destitute hapless persons —often with flawed faces &/or bodies, for want of the barest necessities— who traded roofless, foodless lives in exchange for at least 1 year of municipal room & board. Longer than 1 year, for sacrificial persons kept on reserve for an emergency calamity, such as floods, droughts, or the plague.

Allegedly, women & female animals were exempt from sacrifice. —Perhaps because the formerly sacred female expression of life had become impure, as female deities were replaced by gods.— But this allegation is denied by the blatant sacrifice of Iphigeneia (on which Odysseus insisted) when the Greek fleet was beached at Aulis.

Shame-faced poets have shrouded Iphigeneia's last
moments in mystery: A protective cloud descended &
concealed her from her executioners. Or: She herself
slaughtered a she-goat in her stead. Or: She later reappeared, resurrected, as a virgin-priestess officiating on the
island.
It is equally possible that other women & she-goats, cows,
sows were used, but went unmentioned. & that Thargelia
brides had been persons of either sex, depending on the
supply of sacrificial victims.
Who may or may not have been mercifully drugged: There
seems to be a conspiracy of reluctance by poets, historians,
scholars to soil the cradle of western civilization with
detailed accounts of human sacrifice in ancient Greece.

Mounichion 9

The premature stone that was thrown at me 3 mornings
ago badly bruised my left cheek.

Which outrages my attendant. He can't stop talking
about the selfishness of a city-born & raised Athenian,
using me the property of the city of Athens, entrusted to
his conscientious care to carry out a personal Expulsion
Rite 1 whole moon ahead of schedule.

Even though the citizen is an 11-, maybe 12-year-
old slightly cross-eyed sponge diver's daughter. Who
screamed pitifully as he twisted her throwing arm behind
her back, after he promptly caught her.

He has reported her to the municipality, & she'll receive
the punishment that is traditional for molesters of a
Thargelia volunteer: She'll be made to take my place.
—Being a child of the poor, & cross-eyed, designates her

as a more traditional Thargelia victim that I am. — Unless I publicly forgive her, on Expulsion Day morning, & insist on my scheduled sacrifice, absolving her selfishness with my magnanimity.

Which no one in Athens expects a prospective Thargelia victim to do, designated *or* volunteer.

It will make him happy to take care of me for the extra extra-long year, beyond the remaining 26 days of this regular one: my attendant tells me. Beaming. Assuming that I, too, am happy of the postponement. For which I'm paying with the pain in my cheek. A modest price for an extra-long intercalary year of 384 days of continued living in his conscientious care. He hopes the city fathers aren't planning to put me on reserve for an emergency calamity. Or, if they are, he hopes that there will be no emergency calamity.

I sometimes think he exaggerates his duties: As when he severely reprimanded a fat man for stepping on my sunshine, a few days ago, when I sat in the municipal patio, working on a poem. In that miraculous spring light that gives Athenians the illusion of individual immortality.

The fat man had come to acquaint me with the size & color of the stone he had selected a deep gold topaze, shaped like a baby fist which he wants me to recognize when he aims it at the region of my heart on Expulsion Day. He hopes to regain the affection of his wife of 28 years, who refuses to let him touch her, accusing him of growing breasts & turning into a woman.

As a rule men threw their stones at the symbolic groom, & women at the symbolic bride, aiming for those parts of

the sacrificial couple's anatomy that corresponded to the
location of the affliction want/calamity/fear they hoped
to throw away.

But in cases of unrequited affection of marital trouble,
which increased epidemically with the firmer & firmer
establishment of patriarchy men aimed their stones at the
bride (usually her mouth, abdomen, or heart) & women
at the groom (hands, heart, head).

In order to be effective, good aim was important. But
equally important was the selection of the stones. Each
part of the body required a stone of specific color, shape,
& texture.

For concerns of the

HEAD the stone was to be	BLUE or WHITE. ROUND,
	HARD.
	(White marble!)
THROAT & SHOULDERS	PINK, FLAT, SMOOTH.
HANDS & ARMS	WHITE, PLUMP, SHINY.
HEART	GOLD or PURPLE, HEAVY,
	THE SIZE OF A FIST.
STOMACH	GREEN, POROUS,
	OPALESCENT.
INTESTINES	ORANGE, OBLONG, JAGGED.
KIDNEYS & BLADDER	BLACK or BILIOUS GREEN,
	GRAVELLEY, OPAQUE.
REPRODUCTIVE ORGANS	RED, OBLONG or OVAL
	GLISTENING.
THIGHS	YELLOW, LARGE, LUMPY.
CALVES	BLUE, VEINED, KNOBBY.
FEET	CLAY-COLORED, FLAT,
	CLUMPY.

The rich often threw gems, which no one dared pick up
afterwards, for fear of picking up what the rich person had

thrown away. —Illnesses usually, in the case of the rich. Most often gout, which healing women used to treat with meadow saffron, as they had been taught by the moon goddess Circe.

Mounichion 12

The hapless sponge diver's daughter has been handed over to me, to do with as I please. Short of killing her. She's in the room with me now. Sobbing. Except for her left eye which tends to disappear toward the bridge corner of her nose she is quite pretty. Of that androgynous age our older men find so exciting. It permits them to indulge in retrospective narcissism, & to feel wise while gleaning pleasure.

—Older men like my father. Who would have found her cross-eyed look particularly appealing.

I used to watch my father play with his students, when I was 12, going on 13. I became so experienced, I could tell whom he was going to single out for seduction, by the way he'd look at a new student whom he was seeing for the first time. Whom he'd immediately try to impress, male or female, it didn't seem to matter, as long as the student had a certain blurred look around the eyes.

Which I'd practice, in my room, hoping to make myself appealing. Not to be like my mother. Whose sharp eyesight & sharp tongue I had inherited. Whom my father never tried to impress, or seduce, only to appease.

The girl is sobbing, because I'm making her study the stone she threw at me on Mounichion 6, exactly 1 moon ahead of time. It's a quartz, flat, with sharp edges. It

painfully cut my left cheek directly under the eye. & could
have taken my eye out.

She ought to look for a smooth white pebble. Preferably
one that is shaped like a bird's egg, & aim for the bridge
of my nose, when she tries again on the real Expulsion
Day: I tell her. Hinting that I might give her the chance
to try again on Expulsion Day. That I might publicly
forgive her.

She's shaking her head: She'll never throw another stone
at me. She couldn't. She has seen me now. I'm not ugly
like the others.

She is hugging my knees, sobbing for forgiveness. If
she'd seen my face, that morning of Mounichion 6, she'd
never have thrown the stone. Which she threw ahead of
time only because she'd wanted to make sure I took her
special affliction away with me, & had worried that the
crowds would get in the way of her aim if she waited until
the official day.

She wants to become a hetaera: she sobs.

—Childishly unaware that that once lucratively roman-
tic profession, about which she knows from her   perhaps
romantically inclined   father no longer is what it once used
to be.—

& she can't become a hetaera as long as she's cross-eyed:
her father has been discouraging her: She'd better stick to
cleaning sponges.

Her father is a reasonable man: I say. & recognize
another teenage daughter trapped in the myth of her
father's infallibility as I watch a slow smile widen her face
at my mention of him.

There is a heavy salt-water odor about her, betraying
her sponge-cleaning occupation. It's not unpleasant to me,

but I shall pretend that it is, to persuade my attendant to give her a bath & put some fresh clothes on her, even if she's a criminal who is not to be pampered at city expense. As long as she's confined to my presence & I to hers I might as well enjoy the way she looks.

Actually, she's more attractive than I used to be at her age, even after I practiced the blurred look. Had she lived 2 or 3 centuries earlier, her eye would not have prevented her from becoming a hetaera.   —It drifts off toward her nose mainly when she's upset. — & her reasonable father would have encouraged her to learn the alphabet & become proficient in the arts. But now that Athenian women are appreciated mainly as bodies like mares or cows or sows that once-respected, free-spirited profession has become the last alternative to starvation, for a woman. She might as well become a poetess, if she's planning to make a career of humiliation.

Until approximately 1300 BC hetaerae were treated with respect by Greek society. As in the case of courtesans in 17th-century France, it was wit & intelligence more than physical beauty that qualified them for their chosen profession. For which they received a more rigorous education than private women; with an emphasis on poetry & art.
They often set the trends of fashion, like dyeing their hair the color of chestnut, or perfuming the soles of their feet, after smoothing them with pumice stone.
They entertained the prominent of their time women as well as men in houses bought for them by their admirers.
They learned to practice birth control to maintain their freedom, & assembled dowries in preparation for marriage toward the waning of their careers.

—Dowries are vestiges from matrilocal times, when husbands moved into the households of their wives, & co-administered their wives' properties. In those days it was the husbands who arrived wearing new underwear.—

But as men acquired their taste for domination, which began with the domestication of animals, which they gradually extended to the 'domestication' of women, & interestingly to the control of moon-regulated water, hetaerae became social outcasts.

—(Not unlike the word: punk initially instrumental in the sympathetic love magic of fire kindled by friction has come to mean: whore, or hoodlum.)—

Their dress was no longer imitated by fashion-conscious women, but became a tastelessly blatant kind of uniform topped by bright red hair by which they were forced to advertise their trade. They were punished if they were caught wearing a veil, during off-duty hours, which married women had started to wear to advertise their 'honesty'. & if one of them tried to hide her professional hair under a hat, she risked having it torn from her head, together with a fistful of telltale hair.

—Even though Athenians of either sex allegedly disliked hats, which they thought made them prematurely grey, & rarely wore them in fair weather.—

Instead of cultured, often envied free spirits, hetaerae became bodies, rented out to men by men who controlled & lived off their earnings. Futureless bodies, without dowries, whose only chance at marriage was to volunteer as a Thargelia bride.

By the 3rd century BC matrimony had become indispensable in Athens. Also for men, who were expected to marry between 35 & 37. A bachelor of 40 was held in low esteem. As were unmarried women over 18, or childless wives.

Mounichion 14

I've watched wretched couples die outside our city gates on Expulsion Day ever since I was a baby in the arms of my nurse. Whom my parents permitted to take me along, as was the custom for babies in Athens. They were given a pebble to throw, by their nurses. & told where to throw it, & for what calamity. A calamity afflicting the nurse, usually. Who believed that her baby's pebble, thrown in all innocence, & for the sake of another, was more effective than the best-aimed stone she could throw herself.

I used to throw mine at the backs of the brides, because my nurse suffered from backaches.

As I grew up & started to write poems, I began going to the Thargelia by myself. Tossing my stone at the groom, aiming for the head, hoping to toss out our men's growing prejudice against writing/thinking women.

Incurring the subsequent dinner disapproval of my parents. Who felt that it was time I outgrew the primitive mentality crowds share with children.

As a child it never occurred to me that these ugly deformed bodies that often took hours to die might be feeling pain. Later I rationalized that they had been drugged before they set out for their last slow walk to the city gates. & that their wretched agony had not only been rewarded in advance by 1 year of unaccustomed good & acknowledged living. But that it was sweetened by the ecstatic belief that they were taking our burdens upon their uneven shoulders, & away with them into death.

These were still my feelings during the last Thargelia, 333 days ago, as I tried once again to throw out the steadily growing discrimination against my sex.

—We have become excluded from: politics religion

philosophy   poetry & the arts   medicine. & by recent legislation from the ownership of land & cattle. —

By means of a white marble ball the size of a distant full moon, or child's head, which caught the groom in the right temple with unexpectedly felicitous aim, knocking him off his tottering feet.

Which prompted my father to comment, during dinner, on the gratuitous cruelty of gratuitously educated women. Who ought to be stopped from playing word games, & be taught to use their bodies instead. To perform the physical chores at present performed by our slaves. Which would permit these gratuitously educated women to vent their frustrations, while being useful to the economy. It would certainly help to halt the inflationary curve of slave market prices . . .

Which prompted my mother to smile agreement.

It was precisely at this moment that the moon goddess Circe entered my head, & asked me to help her save the moon's place in the sky.

Which was directly related to the social condition of women for which I had thrown my white marble ball earlier that afternoon.

Explaining to me that civilizations periodically depended on the sacrifice of an enlightened individual to rectify collective mistakes & cancel their cumulative effect. A savior, who understood the interdependence of all forms of life, & the need to balance their respective evolutions, involutions, & revolutions.

This time around the savior needed to be a woman: Circe said: to counter-act the threat of universal destruction by fire.

An out-&-out male form of destruction. & final. Unlike the great flood, a female form of destruction, which had occurred during a matriarchal civilization, when a previous imbalance had favored the female pole of life.

When a man had been called upon to preserve the human & animal life forms. One pair of each. An intelligent man, who had understood the interdependence of his own survival with that of all animal species. & whose sacrifice had consisted of labor, not of death. Bloodshed was not required to counter-act destruction by water. Whose built-in female continuity had allowed fresh vegetation to sprout from the muck.

But this time the source of all life would be sealed like a cauterized wound. Unless an intelligent woman, who felt committed to the cause of women —which she understood to be also the cause of universal survival, & thereby also the cause of the moon— offered her life to stay universal final; irrevocable annihilation.

Which Circe convinced me to do.

Which failed to convince my parents, to whom I explained what Circe had explained to me, before I walked out on their dinner, 333 nights ago.

My parents do not believe in divine voices, in people receiving divine commands. They think that people who claim to hear them & obey them are either frauds, hoping to gain notoriety for want of legitimate acclaim, or else slightly demented, usually uneducated wretches.

If my purpose had been to embarrass or offend my parents, I could not have chosen anything more embarrassing or offensive to them than to volunteer as a Thargelia bride, to let myself be stoned to death during the next 'antiquated superstitious mummery'.

I admit it: I had expected the city fathers to laugh in my face, rejecting my offer. Thargelia brides are supposedly

transvestites, to uphold the hypocritical myth of the inviol-
ability of women. Or else they are work-worn hetaerae, or
other futureless creatures. Old slave women too sick &
weak to work. Whereas I am the daughter of the philosopher Hippobotus. I come from a reputable Athenian
family. That may live economically, but is far from poor.
& I am far from ugly. But all 6 city fathers accepted me
readily. In fact: gloatingly. As though they welcomed the
stoning to death of a woman with no bodily flaws, for the
sole flaw of being educated, a poetess with pretensions
toward thought & words.

Which increased my self-sacrificial ardor. & made me
believe Circe's assurance that: my bodily agony would be
blunted by the ecstasy of dying for a worthy cause.

& by chewing laurel leaves, which she promised to
procure for me.

But recently it is the cause & its worthiness that have
become blunted. For the last 7 days my mind has been
nagged with thoughts of pain. The sponge diver's daughter's premature stone has sowed a seed of fear in my flesh.
Fertilized by the continued throbbing in my left cheek.
Which continues to be inflamed, despite the aloe poultices
my attendant conscientiously prepares for me. I have
trouble falling asleep, apprehending the hundreds of stones
 most of them much heavier than the cross-eyed girl's
quartz, thrown with much greater impact that will leap
at me from every angle, in less than 21 days. In 20 days &
10 hours, to be exact.

—Unless I let the cross-eyed girl take my place. As my
attendant & everybody else in Athens expects me to do.

Which is simpler than staging a scene of public forgiving:
on the highest of the 14 municipal steps; unfastening the

pale green string of figs around her neck, refastening them around mine, in defiance of public expectation.

& a shameful thought, even for a mortally frightened poetess.

Who has been talking back to the moon goddess Circe inside her head. Telling the moon goddess that: Their common cause is doomed.
Pointing to her lack of an audience
—even among women. Who have been falling into the slave mentality their fathers/husbands/brothers even their mothers are designing for them: fearful, devious, acquiescent, lazy—
as proof of their inevitable failure. Women aren't worth the martyrdom the moon goddess wants to inflict upon a mortal poetess' cringing flesh.
If we succeed I might be read: the moon goddess tries to bribe me back into submission.
I'm not sure a posthumous audience is worth dying for: I say out loud into the quiet room.
The sponge diver's daughter stirs in her sleep, turning her face to the wall. I look at her: the scrawny embodiment of my temptation to postpone my sacrifice. Wondering if chewing laurel leaves will really numb the pain of so many stones.
& if absence of pain invalidates the sacrifice.

HIPPOBOTUS, Greek philosopher who lived during the 3rd century BC, author of at least 2 known historico-philosophical treatises.

Mounichion 17

I decidedly won't encourage a realistic acting out of the mating ritual. I caught a glimpse of my intended partner this afternoon, in the crowd that gathers to stare wherever I go with my attendant.

—Now also with the cross-eyed girl. Erinna. Who has been much less cross-eyed, in new clean clothes.—

The man looks far worse than the traditional wretches I have watched die during past Thargeliae. Whose helpless abjection I was prepared to accept when I volunteered for the sacrifice.

—Admittedly expecting the city fathers to laugh in my face, rejecting my offer.—

This man is willfully abject. The greed I saw flickering in his eyes as he scanned first me & then Erinna, visibly weighing which of us would make the better bride & the taut mottled skin encasing his bloated face, which betrays his recent abuse of unaccustomed foods & wine, probably also of sex, purchased at city expense   make me shudder at the prospect of even taking his hand during the long slow walk to the city gates.

Although it would be uncharitable of me not to take it. Unworthy of the cause of women & the moon, which is not served by retaliation.

—It might further impair the effectiveness of my sacrifice, which may already be impaired by my continuous chewing of laurel leaves, of which Circe gave me a lifetime supply.—

The repulsive creature will certainly be paralysed with fear, having used up the material rewards that were his reason for volunteering, with no ideal to deflect the pain.

— About which I cannot stop thinking.—   Or else he'll

be so heavily drugged that he won't be able to walk by himself.

Besides, leading greed to its death is precisely what Circe wants me to accomplish by my sacrifice. To put an irrevocable end to the continuous mating of greed with lazy, fearful acquiescence, that is breeding universal annihilation by fire, before the moon falls from the sky.

The moon goddess Circe, the immortal enchantress, a daughter of the sun, is said to live on the island of Aeaea — The Island of Dawn, now lost in geographical conjecture— off the western coast of Italy.
Her palace stands halfway inland, surrounded by a forest. Which grows denser each year as squirrels plant new trees with the nuts & acorns they bury & forget.
It is a peaceable kingdom, in which animals rest or wander about without fighting or eating each other. The moon goddess feeds them all. Sometimes she changes a shorter-lived species into a longer-lived one a dog into a turtle / a man into a parrot/a carp because she is grieved by the death-fear of creatures. Which makes her weep amber tears, like all daughters of the sun.

There is a cemetery on the riverside of the island, surrounded by tall willow trees, in which only female corpses are buried female animals as well as women because the female body must return to its elements: earth & water. Whereas male corpses are wrapped in untanned ox hide & exposed to sun & wind on top of the willow trees, because men & male animals belong to the elements of fire & air.

For over 3000 years the moon goddess Circe has been

known to live in her palace on Aeaea, singing softly as she
weaves, or gathers herbs, or extracts her drugs.

Her hair is long, & so black it looks blue, like a new-moon
night. Her skin is off-white velvet, & her eyes are jungle
green, flecked with sun. She is an unchanging 30 years old.
This is how she came into being, & this is how she continues
to be until her legend's end. A retired immortal on an
unfindable island, worshipped by distant monthly police
records, indicating higher rates of rape-murder-suicide
during full-moon nights.

Mounichion 18

I find myself identifying more & more with the moon
goddess Circe. To the extent of feeling humiliated by what
I think must feel humiliating to her.

To be known mainly as one of many women in the life
of a long-deceased mortal, for instance. —The falcon in
the alleged trio of birdwomen Penelope, the Duck/Circe,
the Falcon/Calypso, the Swan (or Gull) that allegedly
composed the single wife of Odysseus, or Ulysses, the
braggard from Nowhere Ithaca, who sometimes claimed
to be from Crete. The notorious cradle of liars: If a liar
says that he's from Crete, is he telling the truth or is he
lying. . . An angry-haired, bow-legged adventurer with a
velvet voice, whom Circe failed to turn into a pig.

Whom my contemporaries even my female contemporaries have been turning into a hero. The first 'new'
man of our 'new' society. The deceased mortal is being
worshipped like a god, while the immortal moon goddess
is practically forgotten.

—Oblivion may be the only form in which death can come to an immortal. —

Or else she is briefly mentioned as an evil witch.

Even I, a modern philosopher's begrudgingly educated daughter, first heard of Circe as the hungry woman who guilefully delayed the hero Odysseus on his long sentimental journey home. Until I discovered an older account of his adventures concealed behind an amphora of wine. Which my father stores in the room he uses for teaching. & in every other available spot in the house, during the wine-tasting month of Anthesterion.

When I realized that the past had been rewritten to accommodate the present. To validate our new, male-dominated way of thinking by obliterating the accomplishments of women. Especially in medicine, which the moon goddess Circe had first taught to healing women when she made them aware of the virtues of herbs.

It surprised me that my father, an outspoken advocate of the 'new' man —who allegedly uses his brain instead of or at least before using his muscles— would preserve an antiquated document that still acknowledges knowledgeable women. But of course my father wasn't using his hidden source material to vindicate knowledgeable women, whose social demotion he applauds.

My father has always had ambivalent feelings about Odysseus. For whom he has the sedentary admiration of a philosopher for a man of action. & of a cynic for a liar who elevated deceit to an art form. But he resents the cult that has sprung up around the lying man of action who caused the stoning to death of the great philosopher, inventor & poet Palamedes.

—Who had *not* volunteered to be sacrificed. —

Which the current *Odyssey* almost justifies as an act of

revenge. My father uses selected passages from the older
story to give indiscriminately hero-worshipping students
a slightly less acquiescent view of the murder & the
murderer of Palamedes.

—Whose poetry Homer destroyed out of jealousy: my
father claims.—

But he flatly denied the document's existence when I
quoted from it, one evening during dinner several years
ago. When my mother expressed reservations about the
educational value of the *Odyssey*: The story of a wife
weaving in faithful solitude while her husband wandered
from bed to bed until both turned middle-age didn't set
too good an example for the future husbands who came to
seek my father's instruction.

But Penelope hadn't been faithful! I exclaimed joyfully.
There happened to be another account that had her
bedding down in nightly rotation with all the 50 suitors
that had laid siege to her weaving virtue. An older version,
which still considered a middle-aged wife just as desirable
as her middle-aged husband.

—Without the need to wear Aphrodite's notorious
girdle. Which Homer has Penelope borrow, to explain
her middle-aged desirability to the 50 suitors. & to her
returning husband. After he portrays her as a flabby old
woman, juxtaposed to her just-as-old, but lean, relentlessly
desirable returning philanderer. The hero, who is instantly
recognized by his faithful old dog (after 20 years of
absence), who instantly dies of joy. & by his faithful old
nurse, who gives the disguised guest a bath, & almost
faints at the sight of a familiar scar on the guest's left inner
thigh, where little 8-year-old Odysseus had been gored by
a boar tusk.

Odysseus had been plagued by visions of his wife's 50
lovers barring his entrance upon his return: I said. Which

was why he'd been so reluctant to go home, & kept lingering with Circe in her palace on her island.

Wherever had I picked up such old-fashioned irrelevant decadent nonsense: my father pretended to want to know. Knowing very well where he kept it hidden. Behind his wine.

How could I & my mother expect a hero to live by the standards of housewives. The *Odyssey* had not been written for future husbands, but for new men who were learning to live by their wits. In a changing world, whose gods were fading into subjective thought.

I & my mother would be better advised to read women's stories. About the muses, for instance. Who had clipped the wings of the sirens —after the sirens sang to Odysseus that the world is round.— & made them into feather crowns for themselves. Which they had worn in triumph after defeating the sirens in a vocal & instrumental melody contest. It might give both of us an insight into the female character. With its innate gratuitous cruelty. Even against other women.

But the muses weren't relevant any more: I said. The muses had narrated their own fading away.

Into subjective inspiration, I presumed: I said. Which I was going to put to immediate use. I was going to my room to rewrite the melody contest as a chant of female solidarity:

The sirens would trim their wings themselves. Just enough to feather Odysseus. —To whom they had never revealed that the world was round.— Whom the muses had meanwhile anointed with resin. & together the muses & the sirens would burn the new man, before he became an example to husbands. Fathers/brothers/sons. & a threat to women of the future, the present, & even the past, since our knowledge & accomplishments were being stricken from the records.

My father turned the color of rage, & my mother the color of tried patience. I left them that way, facing each other.

I seem to remember that that night, too, the moon had been full. It always seems to be when I speak out, or take action.

The legend of Circe, the immortal sorceress & goddess of the moon, has survived mainly because of an angry-haired, bow-legged mortal with a seductive voice Odysseus whom she failed to turn into a pig.
She failed because the authors of the *Odyssey* did not wish to make their hero project the classical image of gluttony & ridicule. He was the representative of a new male-dominated mentality, the first man to live by his 'wits', in a world whose deities had lost their ubiquity to image & legend, & were beginning to fade into subjective thought. They no longer issued commands, prompting actions that had been fated rather than willed. The 'new' man had a less intimate relationship with his gods, & suffered responsibility as a consequence.
Such a hero could not afford to be seen, pink & bristled, yet with human mind, wallowing next to 45 successfully transformed companions in the sties of a dangerously knowledgeable woman. He had to be given an antidote heavy as an anchor a black-rooted plant with milk-white flowers, which the authors call: Moly.
—Which may have been a wild cyclamen. Which grows

during the waning of the moon, & may therefore be able
to withstand the magic of a moon goddess. Its scent dispells
all spells.

The Odyssey is also a unique account of consciousness-
altering drugs, which correspond to drugs in use today.
Circe allegedly supplied Helen
—no longer of Troy: She left the city after its fall, once
again in the company of her initial husband Menelaus. —
with a drug called nē-penthē: No Pain. A 'businessman's
drug' of the order of chorpromazine, which may have
resembled cocaine or rauwolfia. When immortality was
conferred upon the reunited couple, Helen allegedly asked
Circe for a drug that prevented 'the sadness of remembering' old grievances. Which led only to anger & recriminations, & made their deathless state hateful & boring to
them.

Perhaps the drugs which Circe offered to Odysseus & his
companions were hallucinogens, which are known to
prompt animal visions. If so, she was not the man-hating,
castrating temptress, who sapped the manhood of her
lovers. Whom she humiliated by transforming them into
pigs wolves/dogs by means of black magic after she tired
of them —usually after 40 days: her alleged desire span—
but a wise & caring woman who may have tried to avert
Odysseus' bloody destiny, his commitment to violence &
deceit, with the potions she extracted from her herbs.

Perhaps Circe was the forerunner of the white witch that
was later persecuted as being possessed by the devil. By
outraged patriarchs who feared that, by aiding the needy,
she was undermining the established hierarchies of domi-

nance: Rich over poor   priest over penitent   man over woman.
—Was there ever any form of domination that did not appear god-given to those who possessed it?—

Mounichion 21

The girl Erinna is astonishingly well acquainted with the adventures of Odysseus. Whom she calls: Ulysses. As she has heard her sponge-diver father call him.
—With veneration, to judge by the daughter's tone of voice.—
Ulysses, The Thigh. The moon goddess Circe is chuckling inside me. She could give Erinna a good reason for calling Odysseus by that name   —a long list of lovers, including Circe herself—   other than the reason the sponge diver gave his daughter: That Ulysses had been gored in the   inner left   thigh by the tusk of a boar when still a child.
For which he never ceased to blame his father. Whom he hated. Laertes, The Ant: he used to call him. Laertes, that Crawling Insect. He never forgave his father for exposing his tender boyhood to an encounter with a boar.
Like other ruthless adventurers, Odysseus treasured tender sentiments about himself as a child. He used to show his scar to the moon goddess Circe & ask her to kiss it.
Circe, & all the other women in his life, probably, beginning with his doting old nurse.
I'm suppressing Circe's temptation to tell Erinna to tell her sponge-diver father   whose echo she seems to be   that

their Ulysses sicked dogs on his aging father, driving him from the house to take his place.

& that he hated the sea   the provider of Erinna's father's livelihood   because of his many shipwrecks. Which he had brought upon himself. Which were his punishment, inflicted by the sea god Poseidon, whose one-eyed son Polyphemus Odysseus had blinded. & afterwards mocked.

Which she would probably refuse to believe. Or else ask her father to justify away.

If she's allowed to see her father while she's a municipal prisoner. Imprisoned in & by my company. My attendant had wanted to keep the girl chained to the wall by her ankles, when he first brought her in.   — There are 2 large rings sunk into the wall, tantalizingly near the entrance, for chaining the ankles of recruited sacrificial victims.—

But he finally agreed that my constant presence was keeping her safe enough.

I've since then drawn a chart above the rings on the wall, for Erinna to exercise her eyes, according to instructions from the moon goddess Circe: A bright-yellow full moon, equally divided into 6 sections by 6 black lines which end in a blunt black circle on the periphery. There is another small black circle in the center of the full moon, with which she must align the tip of her nose before slowly rotating her eyes, 6 times to the right, & 6 times to the left, focusing on the 6 blunt points   or circles   on the periphery. Starting with the top point   or circle   & returning to it to pause for a blink between rotations.

I have trouble convincing the girl that Odysseus & Ulysses are one & the same person. Whose insatiable curiosity plunged him into actions which then led to remorse, or retribution.

She might try to think of the 2 names as the 2 sides of a coin: I tell her: Ulysses standing for the man's achievements, his courage & flexible mind, & Odysseus for his crimes.

Crimes? she repeats after me, her voice faltering. The left eye begins to flee toward her nose. Her father never told her of any CRIMES.

Deceits then: I say with a twinge of moon-goddess irritation. Deceit as a means of survival.

Her father never told her about DECEITS.

Her father may not know everything. Odysseus had LIVED by deceit.

& he'd had a despicable character. He was boastful, had to be the best in everything he tried, & couldn't take criticism. He was a self-serious, self-sentimental, humorless, gloomy adventurer who elevated deceit to an art form.

Erinna has started to cry, but Circe & I ignore it. The girl is of hero-worshipping age she is 12, not 11 & completely blinded by her father's notions, yet her misinformed adulation is beginning to annoy us. Circe suggests that I write a poem listing Odysseus' major misdeeds & deceits. To which I shall force Erinna to listen, since I may do with her as I please, short of killing her.

Meanwhile I might avenge the moon goddess within me by telling Erinna that, if I were her hero Odysseus-Ulysses, I would not hesitate for a moment to let her take my place at the upcoming Thargelia. As everyone expects me to do. Which would give her 14 more days to live. Instead of planning to forgive her, in 14 days, on the first of the 14 municipal steps, before a crowd of incredulous Athenians, before taking or not taking the hand of my repulsive partner, before setting out on my long slow last walk to the city gates.

Instead of thinking up reasons to persuade my attendant

to persuade the city fathers to have the girl sent home to be imprisoned by her father, for those remaining 14 days.

To have her brought back on the eve of Thargelion 6. Which I say only to make my attendant continue to think what everyone thinks: That I'm only too glad to spend my bonus year —an extra-long intercalary year: of 384 days— in his excellent care. At the expense of my 12-year-old molester.

The girl's constant presence in the room has been disturbing my poetic concentration: I've been telling my attendant.

It has, although not as much as it has been disturbing my attendant's sense of humor. He hates the girl. Whose side I've been taking against his and my better judgment when she tries to take over his various chores.

—Like grabbing a hot stone from him burning herself before he can drop it into the water to heat my bath.

Which she does because her infallible father has told her that domestic chores are women's chores. Ennobling for them, but degrading for men.

Which shocks me, at the thought that all the women in Athens must be sharing the girl's unquestioning subservience to the words of their fathers husbands brothers. Since fads of dress as much as of morality start at the social top & trickle down to the lowly. Such as fishermen & sponge divers, & other free Athenians earning a scanty living doing physical labor.

& makes me question the effectiveness of the years of stones —even last year's felicitously aimed white marble ball— I tossed at the heads of Thargelia grooms.

Why am I doing this? I ask myself. & Circe. If it's to be all for naught it might be accomplished just as well by a

12-year-old girl. Why can't Circe leave me alone, & switch over to Erinna?

Who persists in making a slavish nuisance of herself. Even after I tell her: Stop!

To go to the chart I drew for her, & start rolling her eyes: 6 times to the right, & 6 times to the left. Doesn't she want to stop being cross-eyed? Wasn't that why she threw her premature quartz in my face 15 days ago?

While I take my bath.
& tell her & my attendant about Elpenor. The only one among Odysseus-Ulysses' 45 companions who had been grateful to the moon goddess Circe for her hospitality.

Who had enjoyed living on her peaceable island so much, he had let himself roll off the roof of her palace & die, rather than resume an errant existence for the sake of another man's epic. When the impatience of the other 44 companions had finally pressured Odysseus-Ulysses into leaving Circe & her island.

Elpenor had grown attached to one of the moon goddess' maids, & liked to dress up in the maid's clothes & do the maid's chores. Proclaiming that he was Diacchus: one half Diana, & one half Bacchus, after he'd drunk more than one cup of the moon goddess' wine.

Which contained a sweet-tasting, aromatic truth serum. Which made Elpenor understand the dual principle of life. In all of us. & the absurdity of making value distinctions instead of simple differentiations between men & women. & their chores.

Anything well done is ennobling to the doer: I say.

Hoping to appease my attendant. Who interprets

Erinna's meddling with his work as criticism of his conscientious efforts on my behalf.

& as competition for my attention. He hasn't had a
moment alone with me since Erinna's arrival, 15 days ago.
Which disturbs him most of all. He'd gladly thrash her if
I didn't intervene.

I'd let him if I thought a good thrashing might upheave
the modern slave mentality so firmly implanted in the 12-
year-old mind of an Athenian sponge diver's daughter.

Sponge diving in ancient Greece was a profession of the
very poor, practiced by men & young women.

—There is a statue in Delphi erected to a nameless sponge
diver & his daughter, who dove into the sea during a
tempest & loosened the anchors of besieging Persian boats.
Setting them adrift to perish in the storm. —

Divers like fishermen slept in makeshift huts on the
shore, amidst piles of nets, baskets, harpoons, & fishing
lines, until cold weather drove them inside the city at
night, into doorless buildings called Leschae, where the
homeless were welcome. Their frugal meals consisted of 1
daily bran bun, 1 onion, sow thistle leaves, mushrooms,
& acorns. A bowl of galaxia barley cooked in milk was
a rare luxury to them. Sometimes they chewed thyme to
cheat their hunger.

—When they weren't eating they used their mouths as
purses. —

It was a meagre, dangerous life, which forced divers to
become extremely observant & inventive. They learned to
watch for a fish named anthias, which they called the

'Sacred Fish' because its presence signalled the absence of sharks in a diving area.

They poured oil upon the waves to make them calm & translucent, to be able to move & see better at sea bottom. They used large pots which they placed over their heads, making sure the pots' edges sank the instant they sank, to give them more air & permit them to stay under water longer.

The gathered sponges were blanched by sprinkling them with salt fish, collected from the rocks. Afterwards they were thoroughly washed & placed in the summer sun to dry, the hollow part facing up.

The more expensive sponges were rendered still whiter by saturating them with sea water or salt froth. Then they were exposed to the rays of the moon during a succession of calm summer nights.

Other professions of the poor, often practiced also by women, were:

Breadsellers. Who carried their merchandise through the streets piled high on trays.

Flutists. Often hired for parties, sometimes paid by the city during ceremonies.

Vegetable pickers.

Hired laborers.

All physical labor was held in contempt in 3rd-century BC Athens.

Mounichion 23

Commanding the attention of one's fellow citizens is a
gratifying experience. Of which I've become keenly aware
since the first day of my 1-year lifespan as a Thargelia
bride. In the more than conscientious care of my more
than attentive attendant. & I've asked myself if it may
not be this public acknowledgement of one's being
—bordering on love— more than the year of unaccustomed creature comforts that may prompt many a Thargelia volunteer to offer up ignored, short-changed lives.
   —With the exception of my intended groom, the repulsive creature, to judge by the way he looks. By the way he
looked first at me, & then at Erinna, practically undressing
us with his greed-bulged eyes.—
   But last night this unaccustomed acknowledgement of
my person —bordering on love— overwhelmed me
when I became the sudden object of the gratifying attention
of my mother.
   From whom my attendant brought me a message.
   It was quite late. The girl Erinna had long gone to sleep
after unenthusiastically rolling her eyes. & I was sitting
with an amphora of new wine, beginning to work on the
poem the moon goddess Circe wishes me to write about
Erinna's hero Ulysses.
   Which I began to write in the first person, as though I
were the moon goddess Circe, writing her memoirs.
   It was at this point that my attendant entered, ceremoni-
ously handing me my mother's message.
   I was surprised to hear from my mother, from whom I
had not heard in 342 days. & curious to read what she
wished to communicate to me, when we had so rarely
communicated in each other's presence. But my attendant
lingered in the room, re-expressing his joy at the prospect

of taking care of me —alone— for the extra, extra-long
year (of 384 days), after she —indicating the sleeping
girl with his chin— received her just punishment on
Expulsion Day.

In exactly 11 days, & 11½ hours: he said with satisfaction.

It was only after I re-expressed the wish that he ask the
city fathers to have the girl sent home, to be imprisoned
by her sponge-diver father, & ennobled by sponge cleaning
& other womanly chores until Expulsion Day, that he
remembered a pressing errand & hurried from the room.

It is my one request he has not hastened to fulfill. Not
because he remotely imagines that I might intend to die
when I can live another glorious, extra-long year in his
conscientious care. & he is certainly more impatient than
I to be rid of Erinna, but he is an employee of the city, &
he distrusts the working poor. Whose preference for
freedom over security fills him with suspicion. He's afraid
that the girl will disappear among the nets, & baskets, &
other 12-year-olds of the fishing population. That her
father will keep her concealed from municipal justice, &
that she'll be unfindable when he sends his underlings to
fetch her back on the eve of her scheduled punishment.

My mother's message is written with care. & slanted
toward humor. Based I assume on one of my father's
frequent dinner precepts that: Violence is rooted in self-
seriousness. Therefore: Making your potential murderer
laugh might save your life.

To make me laugh at her, at my father, & ultimately
mostly at myself, & make me regret my self-serious, self-
sacrificial impulse

'the pain of which I had either not imagined, or else

cloaked in imaginings of ecstasy . . .', which touches me, coming from my mother

she starts out by recounting or inventing a recent dinner conversation between my father & her. Of which I become the eventual subject. As I have become almost nightly, since my 'impulsive departure': she tells me. Deploring: 'My willful isolation that prevented me from telling her or my father what was really going on in my head. From giving my religious or whatever experience I was going through the benefit of philosophical doubt . . .

'Lust for anything but wisdom & serenity uglifies old flesh. & if the musk of its decay attracts youthful lovers, they are like flies on a corpse': she has herself saying at the outset. In her usual dinnertime derision of my father's unphilosophical abuse of his easy access to the student body to whom he teaches philosophy.

To which she has my father replying —true to character; I practically heard him speak— that: 'The seed of wisdom though probably not of serenity; of ataraxia, the freedom from vanity & self-conceit could be sowed in many ways. Including the biological shortcut, since old-age fertility was an incontestable male prerogative. As incontestable as wisdom.

'& . . .' —this is where I come in as the subject— 'a more constructive approach to posterity than the full-moon urge of a bodily healthy, & otherwise not disadvantaged 30-year-old poetess to volunteer as a fig-tree bride.

'Which was not going to gain her a posthumous audience. No one in Athens cared to hear a 30-year-old woman complain about being a woman. Not even if she looked exquisite as a corpse, & her collected works were found in her cleavage.'

The message ends with my mother's offer to supply me with hemlock. 'A reliable poison which is known to cause a gradual numbing of the body's functions & sensations, beginning with the feet & slowly traveling upwards to the heart. A slow, allegedly painless withdrawal of life, which would permit me to die in the relative comfort of my municipal bed. & in dignified solitude.

Without diminishing my sacrifice. I'd still be dying for my worthy cause. Which was admirable of me. Giving my life so that future generations of women might live equally again.

Dying with dignity would actually serve the cause of women better. Without adding the sting of ridicule — that had become associated with agonizing *pharmakoi*, appointed *or* voluntary— to the agony of my poor lapidated flesh.

Which, moreover, risked looking indecent, exposed to torture . . .'

I could feel Circe bristling inside me while I read. & as soon as the message ended, she burst into vehement disagreement with my mother's recommendation of a private dignified death.

Which completely defeated our purpose, serving neither the cause of women nor the cause of the moon. I might as well go on living. & let the 12-year-old girl take my place: she said hotly.

Ridicule was an important part of sacrifice! It dehumanized the victim. Why did I think the City of Athens a city renowned for her emphasis on physical beauty recruited traditional Thargelia couples from among the naturally disadvantaged? Because hunched backs, & crossing eyes, & uneven legs made the normal citizen laugh. Because those limping, cross-eyed hunchbacks were different. Ugly. Which made the normal citizen think that they didn't feel pain like normal citizens, because their ridiculous bodies made a mockery of suffering. Which the normal citizens would otherwise not be able to watch. & still less to inflict.

Continuing instead to inflict unspectacular daily pains upon each other. Whose cumulative effect was sure to throw the universe off balance. Until the moon fell from the sky.

When had I ever listened to my mother before? she asked, sounding disgusted.

But I was moved that my mother cared enough about my pains-to-come to recommend suicide. Which my father had always dismissed as: an act of courage for lack of courage. & blamed on self-seriousness, & self-dramatics. Especially in the case of women who preferred death to being raped. Even by Apollo.

& never before had my mother seemed to be concerned with the deteriorating condition of women in our city. Only with my father's profiting from that condition.

Of course her message may have been dictated by embarrassment. Her own &/or my father's. Who may be trying to stop his daughter from starring in a role that is traditionally played by the destitute-prostitute-&/or crippled. Although I had rather expected my father to turn the public spectacle of his embarrassingly self-sacrificial daughter into a source for epigrams with which to dazzle his students. For theories about the behavior of gratuitously educated women . . . of 30 . . . childless . . . without a husband . . . still living under their parents' roof . . . writing poems . . .

Somehow I had dismissed the thought of my parents. I had lived like a boarder in their house. & when I walked out, a little over 11½ months ago, I thought that they would simply cease having a daughter.

I went to sleep with my mother's message on my mind. & it was still on my mind when I woke up.

To whispers coming from Erinna's corner of the room. & a tickling in my nostrils, caused by an intense odor of salt water. In the milky twilight that precedes the Athenian dawn during the month of Mounichion (March 28 to April 27, during regular years of 354 days) in the early hour immediately before daybreak, when the city holds its funerals, I distinguished a wildly gesturing male figure bending over Erinna's bed.

—On arched bare legs, the sight of which made me think of Circe's lover Odysseus about whom I had started writing the evening before. Who had been notoriously bow-legged, according to Circe.—

I watched the figure pull the girl to her feet, her white-robed androgynous body melting into his, before I inquired: With whom we might be having the honor, at this early hour of a new spring day, when the only people about in the streets were old women dressing corpses for burial.

In my most honeyed voice, hypocrisy being the homage intellect pays to custom. —Female intellect to recent male supremacy.— Whatever custom may require of a 30-year-old Athenian poetess without an audience, addressing a bow-legged male intruder in the special chamber the municipality reserves for voluntary Thargelia brides.

That she disguise her apprehension, I imagine. & sound politely in control, regardless of the identity of the intruder —who might after all be one of the city fathers— or the nature of his quest.

For a moment I thought that my repulsive Thargelia groom who enjoys the same privileges I enjoy had passed unhindered through the flight of municipal halls that separate the grooms' chamber from ours.

That he had been allowed to enter our chamber by my conscientious attendant, upon the assurance that he had not come for me, but for the cross-eyed girl. Whom my attendant hates. Who needed to rehearse the mating ritual of 2 fig trees nightly from now on if they were to achieve credibility as a couple during the symbolic moment.

Because he preferred Erinna's androgyny to my fullness, after checking us out in the street, with his greed-bulged eyes.

Or because he really wished to rehearse the mating ritual, & the thought that I might forgive Erinna, that I might be his bride after all, had never crossed his repulsive mind.

Or simply because Erinna's cot happened to be nearer to the entrance.

But the bow-legged shadow figure whom my voice interrupted in the motion of slinging Erinna over his left shoulder did not repulse me, even if he made the room smell as though we were being marinated in brine.

& the deep caressing voice that was returning my hypocrisy again made me think of Circe's mortal one-time lover, as the intruder said: That the honor was entirely his, being but a humble diver for sponges in a city that despised physical labor.

He felt deeply honored to be in the presence of a lady who was as learned as she was beautiful: he said.

How could he tell? It was still quite dark: I laughed. Remembering a long-ago evening in my parents' house when I had overheard my father's courtship voice telling a wine-bearing slave girl 'how her beauty increased as the light faded'. & the girl answering with audacious wit, it had seemed to me; made audacious & witty by the promise she'd heard in my father's voice, perhaps; unless she was serious & dumb: That my father ought to see her on a moonless night. That she looked perfect then.

I hadn't dared to laugh at it at the time. My mother had been sitting in the room with me, & she refused to look up when I tried to meet her eyes, to exchange at least a smile. My father has never been a smiling matter to my mother.

& how did he know that I was learned? I asked. Had he heard my poems?

No, he had not had that opportunity. But he knew that I was the daughter of a learned philosopher. & he had seen me. On the day of his dishonor. Of his shame, when his Erinna had hurt me with her impatient stone. For fear of staying cross-eyed all of her life.

For which she deserved punishment, certainly. But perhaps not the harsh punishment that was traditional for adult molesters of Thargelia volunteers. But had never before been applied to a teeange offender. A mere child. By the city fathers, who had forgotten how time felt to a 12-year-old. Who was cross-eyed. & desperate for a miracle.

His daughter's life was in my merciful hands: he said, setting the girl back on her feet. After all, I had chosen to be a Thargelia bride. Out of compassion for my fellow citizens, he presumed, since he could detect no outward selfish reason for my wishing to sacrifice a flawless body. & condemn it to death. Surely, one extra year couldn't be worth another's life to a compassionate, self-sacrificing, beautiful, learned woman who wrote poetry. A 12-year-old life that hadn't had the time to learn from its experience.

I felt despair behind his flattery. The determination to

cajole or shame me into saving his daughter's life by publicly forgiving her. & deep love for his daughter behind his desperate determination. So different, in its animal urgency, from my mother's carefully humorous invitation to suicide, or my father's philosophy of laughter. At the expense of others.

I also felt the bruise on my cheek. With my fingertips, making it hurt.

Wasn't every mortal's death a matter merely of time? I asked, prompted by Circe. Further sweetening my honey voice. & wasn't the experience of death supposed to teach the dying all they needed to know about life, regardless of age?

Besides, the extra year he wanted me to sacrifice happened to be an intercalary extra-long year: of 384 days.

& how had he managed to enter our chamber to steal his daughter I presumed undetected by our ever-vigilant attendant. Who never slept.

Whom I would summon this instant, to assure myself that the conscientious municipal servant had not come to harm, as a result of the sponge diver's intrusion.

& to inform him that I intended to purchase 3 large sponges for my baths.

& to ask him to serve all 3 of us a herb tea a mixture of chamomile & rauwolfia, which warmed the heart & sedated sorrow. Which the moon goddess Circe had served to one of her guests. The man whom his daughter & he, I presumed called: Ulysses. Which we would drink while we discussed the price of sponges.

The Athenian Calendar

was based on the moon. Which takes 29 days, 12 hours, 44 minutes, & 2.8 seconds to complete its monthly cycle. Each month began with the actual observation of the new lunar crescent, although officially a 'full' month of 30 days alternated with a 'hollow' month of 29 days.

A lunar year consisted of 12 lunations, or: 354 days, 8 hours, 48 minutes, & 34 seconds. (To: 365 days, 5 hours, 48 minutes & 46 seconds in a solar year.) The extra hours, minutes & seconds were equalized by counting a regular year as having 354 days, & intercalating 1 year of 355 days every 4 years, & 1 year of 384 days every 16 years, when the 6th month (POSIDEON) was repeated. The second time POSIDEON was counted as a 'full' month of 30 days, instead of its usual 'hollow' 29 days.

The Athenian year began on the first day after the summer solstice, when the crescent of the new moon became visible. It was divided into 2 seasons: the season of the OX (summer), & the season of the ASS (winter), respectively representing Zeus & Cronos —Jupiter & Saturn, respectively the planet of beneficence & the planet of restriction. The beginning date given for each month is an approximation, taken from an intercalary year of 384 days. During regular years of 354 days & the minor intercalaries of 355 days, it falls 30 or 29 days earlier.

	Corresponding Date	Number of Days
1) HEKATOMBAION	from July 6	30
2) METAGEITNION*	from August 6	29
3) BOEDROMION	from September 3	30
4) PYANEPSION	from October 1	29
5) MAIMAKTERION	from November 1	30

6) POSIDEON	from December 1	29
POSIDEON II	from December 30	30
7) GAMELION**	from January 29	30
8) ANTHESTERION***	from February 28	29
9) ELAPHEBOLION	from March 29	30
10) MOUNICHION	from April 28	29
11) THARGELION****	from May 27	30
12) SKIROPHORION	from June 26	29

*METAGEITNION, the month for 'changing neighbors'.
**GAMELION, the month for marrying. —The marriage of Hera & Zeus was celebrated on the 26.— Marriages contracted during the full moon had the best chance for happiness & duration.
***ANTHESTERION, the month for tasting new wine.
****THARGELION, a month of festivals. The 4th was dedicated to Apollo.

The 6th was EXPULSION DAY: driving out of evil, purification rites & (human) sacrifice.
The 7th: Offerings of fruits to implore the ripening of the harvest.

Mounichion 25

The power to hurt is an attribute of the divine —the reverse side of the power to bestow blessings— & sometimes goddesses & gods succumb to the temptation of using it, in the name of retribution & subsequent enlightenment. Feeling divine compassion for victims who placed themselves in their vulnerable positions, through negligence, laziness or ambition.

But in the hands of mortals the temptation to use the hurtful power can turn into compulsion, unmitigated by

compassion. Making men feel godly as they spread pain &
sorrow. Which they call: the human condition. For others.
Which they hope to avoid for themselves by passing it on
to others. Thus maintaining its existence: Making misery
immortal.

Which is not what I wish to do. Not even to immortalize
my unheard poems.

I've been praying to the moon goddess Circe inside my
head to help me withstand the mortal temptation to
use my inadvertently, & therefore innocently acquired
sudden power to hurt the sponge diver's cross-eyed
daughter.

& the sponge diver, directly &/or through his cross-eyed
daughter.

Who literally threw the sudden power to hurt her in my
face, 19 days ago. Placing herself & her father, after he
unlawfully entered my life in the milky pre-dawn twilight
of Mounichion 19, when he scaled the wall of my municipal
bridal chamber building in their vulnerable positions.

Causing a bruise on my left cheek, that still feels
painful to the touch of fingertips, despite my conscientious
applications of the aloe poultices my attendant conscientiously prepares for me.

But the moon goddess Circe inside my head is reluctant
to help me decide between my continued living one extra
 extra-long year at Athen's expense, & saving the 12-
year-long life of my molester.

She has been offended by the sponge diver's worship of
a one-time lover of hers, a gloomy, ambitious, self-serious
mortal long since deceased, but whose increasingly flatter-
ing epic continues to stir the imagination of men.

Even of men as lowly & uneducated as an Athenian
sponge diver. Who has contaminated his cross-eyed daugh-

ter's 12-year-old imagination with his hero worship, while telling the girl next to nothing about the moon goddess Circe.

Which makes the immortal goddess feel almost dead, for want of believers. Forgotten: Which is the only form death dares to take, in the case of immortals.

The moon goddess has no reason nor perhaps the power to save the life of a cross-eyed 12-year-old sponge diver's daughter who, until recently, knew next to nothing about her. & may therefore not believe in her. Making it impossible for the immortal moon goddess to come to her aid.

On the other hand, the sponge diver's misplaced worship increases the moon goddess' concern for the fate of humanity. Whose extinction would also extinguish all memory of immortal moon goddesses & worship-unworthy mortal diehards, by implicating the fate of the earth. In turn implicating the fate of the moon.

Which increases the moon goddess' reason for wanting to sacrifice my fine-minded/healthy/shapely-body-in-its-prime. Which she borrowed for that purpose 344 days ago, on the evening after the last Thargelia. After borrowing my right hand normally used for writing poems earlier that same afternoon, to throw a white marble ball the size of a distant full moon, or child's head, at the head of the Thargelia groom. To throw out the increasing disregard for the thoughts & deeds of women in general, & for audienceless poetesses in Athens in particular.

In the course of the last 344 days the moon goddess Circe & I have become almost interchangeable.

& we have taken the sponge diver for our lover.

Which needs no justification. & still less an apology.

— Not even the apology for female acquiescence to male

greed: My Circe-filled body & its sponge-diver lover have
been sharing equally in the give & take of lust. —
A voluntary Thargelia bride may indulge in all her
whims, short of escaping. Or raping the voluntary groom.
A whim, but not a serious involvement. A public figure
living at city expense is not expected to have a private life.
Which I never had before. Which further complicates
my impending decision. I hesitate to give up a life I've just
begun to enjoy.

The imbalance between the female & the male principles
of life began as a love play between Metis, the goddess of
Wisdom, & the ever-amorous Zeus.
—Before he married his twin sister, Hera, & began the
immortal conjugal battle that established monogamy in
Greece, & became the model for nagging wives & philandering husbands. —

Metis was pregnant, & Zeus feared that, if Wisdom bore
his child, he would be deposed. Just as he had deposed his
own father.
—Chronos. Who had swallowed Zeus' older brothers, but
failed to swallow Zeus. Swallowing instead a plump stone
wrapped in swaddling cloths. —
Zeus lured Metis to a couch, & convinced her with kisses
& caresses to let him shrink her into a fly, so that he might
swallow her. Perhaps the thought of being inside her lover
excited Metis. Who never suspected in her never-before-
contested wisdom; which may not necessarily include
love-play psychology that Zeus' demonstrations of all-
engulfing passion might have an ulterior motive: such as

preventing the birth of a successor while incorporating his lover's wisdom.
—Which he then proceeded to claim for himself.
Wisdom used to be an innately female quality, derived from the moon. Whose reflective non-burning light grants or denies water to the fields, & children to women's wombs. It is a wisdom of flux of continuity in change
 (the name: Metis means change; same root as Moon)
 that acknowledges neither rank nor competition. Like water, it flows on & nowhere piles up.
But after Zeus swallowed Metis, men began claiming wisdom as their own exclusive attribute.
—As well as the control of moon-regulated, life-controlling water, which men took over at the beginning of agriculture, during the Taurean age. —
Perverting wisdom to fit their own solid natures:
There are accounts of early priests, wearing sharp metal claws on their left little fingers, with which they wounded themselves beneath their newly borrowed robes,* to

*During the 3rd century BC the average Athenian wore unisex tunics, which stopped at the knee. Ankle-long robes had been the official dress of priestesses & earlier female rulers.

—Who often allowed their consorts or lovers to borrow the robe(s) that represented their office, & deputize for them.
The Lydian Queen Omphale, who had bought Heracles on the slave market knowing a bargain when she saw one derived great satisfaction from dressing his super-masculine body in her gold-embroidered robes, turban, purple shawl, jewelled necklaces & bracelets, & watch him spin amidst the women of her court, or conduct state business while she stood by. —

As men began taking over more & more offices initially held by women, they took over the women's robes as well.

simulate a flow of monthly blood, as they sat on tripods of replaced priestesses, during drug-induced periods of prophecy.

& Odysseus, the first man to live by wit rather than muscle, dried wisdom up to shrewdness, using it mainly to deceive.

You are what you eat. In his greed to ingest wisdom Zeus ultimately ate a fly.

It gave him a divine headache, from which burst forth his pugnaciously virginal daughter Athena. It is the only case of male parthenogenesis on record.

Since then, men have been feeling wise by turning women into flighty little creatures, too insignificant to be allowed to share in the government of life.

Woman is but a furrow for man to sow his seed: was the argument used by Apollo, which acquitted Orestes of matricide during the murderer's trial in Athens.

This also applies to trousers
—which originated in the East (where the sun also rises), as did the later solar Greek deities (Apollo)—
which were originally worn exclusively by Eastern women, & considered unsuitable for the male anatomy. But as men began wearing the pants
—which the dictates of nature-defying fashion moulded more & more clinging, to show off the anatomy they were constricting—
the irritated, exasperated genitals were forced into constant sexual awareness. Which made men resent the women whose offices they were taking over, with their dress.

This may account for many instances of rape & other forms of sex-related violence. Although cases of divine rape in Greek mythology occurred during pre-trouser times, at the beginning of patriarchy, when earlier lunar deities were replaced by sun gods like Zeus —who preferred persuasion or deceit to violence— & Apollo —who was impatient, & very direct.

Shockingly seconded by the motherless Athena.
Women siding with men in the belittling of women became
common practice after the rape of their wisdom.

Mounichion 26

It isn't easy to conduct a love affair under the reproachful
gazes of my attendant & my lover's ever-present daughter.

Erinna is insanely possessive of her father, who raised
her from her first moment on this earth, since the mother
died in childbirth.

Their attachment stung me with envy, at first, compared
to my father's philosophically condescending banter, &
my mother's carefully humorous concern, leading up to
her offer to supply me with the means of suicide. But I
quickly got over my unworthy emotion when I saw it
mirrored in the reproachful eyes of Erinna & my attendant.

Who can do nothing to stop me from inviting the sponge
diver to my municipal bridal chamber. His first duty is to
fulfill my wishes. Short of letting me escape. Which is
impossible anyway, even if I disguised myself. As a man,
or maybe as an old woman. Athens has no hiding places
for recanting Thargelia volunteers. At least not the Athens
I know. The 'respectable' Athens. For another 8 days my
attendant will have to let my lover share my meals, my
wine. My bed. Whatever, whenever I wish.

—Plus for the extra, extra-long year, if I enjoy my
life with the father too much to choose to forgive his
daughter.—

He peevishly takes Erinna by the hand —He likes her
better now, that they have the common goal to keep her
father & me apart.— to run the errands I send them on.

With detailed instructions: To fetch a cool amphora of new wine & delicately marinated mussels & freshly baked bread.

Take your time: I tell them with a wink: Don't run your errands. Walk them.

They nod. Gazing reproachfully from me to the patiently impatient sponge diver, & back to me, their eyes projecting exaggerated images of intertwined bodies.

I'm aware that the sponge diver had more than one reason to become my lover. Just as his hero Ulysses

—after whom he tries to model himself. At least in his conduct with me, not with Erinna. Ulysses had no daughter, & he showed no paternal concern to any of his sons—

had more than one reason to become the lover of the moon goddess Circe. Reasons calculated by fear, the psychological antithesis of love. However, just as in the case of his hero's involvement with my moon goddess, his desire for me has become as pure as crystal. Pure, unmitigated lust, which the grateful flesh translates into love.

As my flesh is about to do. I was a virgin still, at 30. An iron butterfly, encased in a cocoon of unshared poems. & paternal philosophy. Which kept fogging up my head like the collective bad breath of yawning audiences. But the moon goddess guided my inexperience, & I exult in the 2-way possession of a man bewitched.

A simple man, without what Athenians call learning. But who conducted himself with greater courtesy than my learned father, who paid us a surprise visit this afternoon. Entering my municipal bridal chamber unannounced since my attendant was absent, running an errand with Erinna.

My father had hardly expected to find me in what he called: an animal posture. & inquired: If I wasn't pushing my self-sacrificial impulse a bit far, letting a fisherman dive for my pearl.

He is an intellectual snob, disgustingly smug within the cloak of his acquired knowledge. His condescension toward my lover touched upon rudeness. He was not speaking to one of his adoring students, but to a mature man, barely a decade younger than he, & my guest. & thereby also the guest of the City of Athens.

It gave me a gleeful satisfaction to compare the sponge diver's elegant leanness & easy play of muscles to my father's column-like middle & rigidity.

& to suggest that the two engage in a contest. Which would permit each man to stand his own ground while respecting the ground of the other.

The contest was to consist of 2 phases.

In PHASE I, the learned philosopher would arm-wrestle with my lover. —Who, incidentally, was neither a fisherman nor a pearl diver, but a diver for sponges.

In PHASE II, the winner would uphold the virtues of Odysseus/Ulysses against counter-arguments from the loser. —My father. Who would know how to crush my lover's enthusiastic emulation of the murderer of the great philosopher Palamedes. Unwittingly avenging the moon goddess Circe.

Under my impartial arbitration.

& before a delighted audience: Erinna & my attendant, who had just then returned. With an amphora of new wine. No mussels, but a sizzling porgy, & aromatic bread.

With which I proposed to celebrate the outcome of the contest.

My lover smiled agreement. Erinna & my attendant clapped their hands, laughing, visibly relieved that someone had come to disturb the sponge diver's & my intimacy during their absence.

But my father refused to stay. Despite his fondness for new wine, with which he fills every corner of the house during the wine-tasting month of Anthesterion.

I was a changed person: he said. Which proved once again his theory of the biological shortcut to learning. Although, in my case, he had his doubts as to the qualifications of the teacher.

He also announced the impending visit of my mother. Which my mother intended as a surprise to me. However, he thought it better to warn me, as a favor to both of us. My mother might not appreciate walking in on a biological shortcut.

Originally, the word VIRGIN described a woman who chose to live independently rather than commit herself to marriage & childbearing. The original virgin did not necessarily abstain from sex, but if she happened to bear a child it had been fathered by a god.

The lunar goddess Artemis —better known as Diana, less well known as Britomartis— initially was a rustic deity, worshipped as: The Sweet Virgin. She was the predecessor of: Mother Earth. A famous statue of Artemis in Ephesus, W. Asia Minor, depicts her as a goddess of fecundity with 16 breasts, who personifies hidden knowledge.

—The zodiac sign Virgo mutable earth occurs in late August through September 21, immediately following harvest time, when the soil recovers its virginity to rest before being recommitted to new seed. —

With the beginning of agriculture, which brought the gradual dependence of women & militarism in its proprietary wake, the word acquired its current meaning. What used to be the simple description of a condition took on a moral judgment. A woman's unbroken hymen became a synonym of purity
—Just as left & right became gauche & dexterous, or sinister & righteous. (The left foot is still the 'hostile' foot, with which soldiers start their march to war.)—
& 'honest' married women conceived out of duty to society, as sexual pleasure became a male prerogative, a source of glory to men, a source of shame to women.
Accordingly, the pregnancy of the Virgin Mary

—the Christian equivalent of a universal-virgin-mother
  Mary means OCEAN, the moon-controlled female element of water, from which all forms of life on earth are said to have arisen. During the Cancerian age which started approximately 8,300 BC; Cancer is Cardinal Water & ruled by the moon. —

is explained as a parthenogenetic phenomenon. Which dispenses with the notion of a mother having (had) intercourse. An offensive notion to her children; especially to sons.

& the Sweet Virgin Artemis, the 16-breasted goddess of fecundity & secret knowledge, became the stern-browed huntress —(The bitter unwithering herb Amaranth became associated with her.)— as she was pledged to strictest chastity by those who worshipped her. —& by her jealous twin brother Apollo.— The names of former lovers were stricken from her records, & her unerring bow & arrow cruelly punished any man she suspected of coveting her affection. Or of having glimpsed her bathing nudity.

The amorous hunter Acteon was changed into a stag by the outraged virgin goddess, & torn to shreds by his own hounds.

& Apollo tricked her into fatally shooting Orion the only man still mentioned who might have touched her virginity-frozen heart by challenging her to hit a tiny dot that was dancing on the waves far off shore. The dancing dot turned out to be the head of the swimming Orion.

Artemis was an earlier lunar deity, & as such had to be given her share of cruelty which solar theologies ascribed to the moon. Apollo was a sun god, whose newcomer's jealousy could not tolerate any lovers or worshippers of the moon.

Mounichion 28

My mother has come & gone. Delivering
TEN IRREFUTABLE ARGUMENTS
refuting the virtues of the overrated hero
ODYSSEUS

1) O. the Perverted Son   who sicked dogs on his aging father & drove him from his home, which the son then claimed for himself.

2) O. the Coward   who feigned madness to avoid going to war before Troy, for a cause to which he had pledged allegiance.

3) O. the Turncoat   who turned recruiter & dragged Achilles off to that same war, after Palamedes saw through his feigned madness.

4) O. the Sacrilegious   who insisted on the sacrifice of his ally's 20-year-old daughter Iphigeneia when the Greek fleet was beached at Aulis.

5) O. the Savior of His Own Skin   who advised abandoning his companion Philoctetes who had been bitten by a snake.

6) O. the Envious Grudge-Bearer, Vindictive Liar, & Assassin   who falsely accused & devised the death of the great philosopher, inventor, & poet PALAMEDES, who had seen through his feigned madness & forced him to honor his pledge.

7) O. the Impious   who cursed old Priam when he came to beg for the body of his slain son Hector.

8) O. the Godless   who stole the Palladium, Troy's sacred temple image.

9) O. the Child Killer   who caused the assassination of Hector's infant son Astynax, gratuitously, after the fall of Troy.

10) O. the Ingrate   who did not spare old Hecuba, who had spared him when he infiltrated her city.

Which my father had put together immediately upon his return home. Apparently my father welcomes a contest with my lover, as long as he doesn't have to endure the common fisherman's superior bodily presence.

There was an 11th argument to refute the virtues of the overrated Odysseus: I said to my mother: The argument I remembered her using during a long-ago dinner conversation, questioning the wisdom of teaching the Odyssey to future Athenian husbands. O. the Philanderer. Which my father had omitted. Intentionally, perhaps. Perhaps he considered philandering one of O.'s virtues . . .

I was smiling. Expecting her to smile back, in acknowledgement of the mother-daughter understanding I'd thought she'd been trying to establish, with her carefully humorous invitation to suicide.

Which had surprised & moved me.

But her face maintained the blank expression with which she had handed me my father's list.

I had humiliated my father & her, by extension forcing a philosopher, the respected Hippobotus, into a contest with a fisherman: she reproached me, blank-faced & humorless. Re-establishing the total lack of communication between us the instant we were once again in each other's presence.

How can my mother feel humiliated by my love for a man who happens to earn his living by the use of his superior body, when she has felt humiliated all her life at least all of my life, from what I was exposed to witness by my father's abuse of the privileges he derives from his allegedly superior male mind.

Which is superior only insofar as he is able to speak it, which my mother is not able to do. At least not in public. Not any more than I am able to find an audience for my poems.

— Except my recent captive audience, consisting of my molester to whom I may do anything I please, short of killing her & my molester's father, my lover. —

My mother looked too distant, sitting there beside me on my municipal bridal couch, to ask her — prompted by the recent exultation of my flesh— why she had never taken a lover, instead of launching circuitous dinner attacks against my father's fatuous infatuations. She is an interesting woman. & still good looking. Far better looking than my philandering pillar of a father. But then, I, too, am good looking, & the thought of taking a lover had never entered my mind either, during the long adult years I had lingered as a boarder under my parents' roof. Or, if it had, I had hastily repressed it as: trespassing on my father's privileges, by following his example.

I waited for my mother to repeat her offer: to supply me with the means of committing suicide 'as a less painful, yet effective alternative to my sacrifice'. Of 'dying a private death, in the dignity of solitude'.

— Which I sadly realized she had offered solely to spare herself & my father the embarrassment of my public

agony. Which may also have been the reason behind my
father's surprise visit 2 days before. I would have been
grateful to have those means at my disposal none the less.
Just in case. —

But my mother didn't bring it up. & I didn't dare ask
her doubting almost that she had made the offer, that I'd
received her message as I looked at her, sitting distant
beside me, reproaching me for humiliating the respected
philosopher Hippobotus & her, the lawful appendage to
the respected philosopher by taking a common fisherman
for a lover.

Whose professional smell she claimed to detect, lingering on my skin.

Wrinkling her nose. Amply returning the humiliation.
With the parental license to say & do to the children what
the children may not say or do to the parents.

My lover was not a fisherman, he was a diver for sponges:
I smiled. Retracing a recent caress at the base of my neck
at her mention of my skin. Which my lover had said
earlier that morning felt like the ocean on a warm summer
night.

Would she care to see the 3 big beautiful sponges the
City of Athens had bought for my baths, from my lover?
I asked her; sweetly.

No, she did not care to see them. But she did care to
warn me about the mentality of uneducated men. Who
were boastful & devious, by sheer force of circumstances.
My lover was sure to laugh & make vulgar jokes about me
to his own kind. He obviously had ulterior motives for
being my lover.

Yes, he had or had had, at the outset: I nodded. Taking
her aback.

His ulterior motive was standing over there, in the

corner of the room: I said, pointing to Erinna. Who stood, demurely rolling her eyes in front of the chart I drew on the wall for her. Which she likes to do whenever we have visitors. Especially when her father comes to see me. When she also likes to sit down & demurely copy the letters of the alphabet I wrote out for her. Hoping to attract my visitor's her father's attention. Away from me.

Erinna loves attention.
Because she was born on the day of the summer solstice: her father told me. To convince me that his daughter was special worthy of saving when he was still trying to convince me to save his daughter's life. At the cost of 1 extra-long year of mine. Trying to arouse motherly feelings in me for his motherless daughter.

Which he still tries to arouse. Although no longer at the cost of my life. He now tries to convince me to stay alive, for & with him & his motherless daughter. To ask my attendant to take Erinna & me for a stroll along the harbor, on one of my remaining 6 5 4 evenings. The sooner the better. When he & other sponge divers, & a fisherman with a boat will gag my attendant. Gently, before the conscientious man has time to cry out. & tie him up painlessly: at my insistence in a fishing net. & I & Erinna will be placed in the fisherman's boat, that is already waiting in the harbor, & my lover will row us away from Athens, to a far-away island of stoneless bliss.
To Circe's island of Aeaea? I ask. Playing with him. I don't mind playing Circe: I say: As long as he can resist playing gloomy Ulysses.

He knows about the moon goddess now. From my

poems about her. To which I've forced him & Erinna to
listen.

To which Erinna listens eagerly. She prefers listening
to my poems to being sent away on an errand with my
conscientious attendant when her father comes to visit.

I've also forced both of them to listen to my earlier poems
about the steadily deteriorating condition of women. How
all our accomplishments are being obliterated, & attributed
to men.

Which brings a contrite look to my lover's salt-cured
face.

I tease him about it. Would he like to take over my or
his daughter's role at the next Thargelia, in the garb of a
fig-tree bride? I ask. Mourning his own death, dressed as
a woman, as custom permits men in mourning.

Or like the king of old, who was allowed to deputize for
the queen, as long as he wore her robes.

Or simply as a currently traditional Thargelia transvestite. Thereby saving his daughter's life directly. Or mine.
Or perhaps both, if the city fathers accept him as a
susbstitute for his daughter. Whom they scheduled to
substitute for me. Unless I publicly forgive her.

If nothing else, it would save our few remaining 5 4 3
days from further endless discussions about my impending
choice. From his pressuring me to ask my attendant to
take Erinna & me on our elopement stroll to the harbor.
Against my better judgment.

His plan is bound to fail, even if it succeeds: I say to
him. Laughing: Is there life outside of Athens? I ask.
Every trend is set in Athens. Even the trend of the
domestication of women.

Even the moon goddess Circe was forced to leave her
island of Aeaea, & come to Athens, in her attempt to save
the moon's place in the sky . . .

I keep teasing him. Aware of my cruelty. Against which I've been praying to the moon goddess Circe inside my head. But I've never been loved before, & it is tempting to test the strength of love through pain.

For which I'll be paying several hundred fold, in 7 short days. When I publicly forgive Erinna, on the highest of the 14 municipal steps. & immortalize her father's love for me by my martyrdom. At least for as long as he lives.

Unless his love for me turns to hate, if I don't forgive Erinna. If I choose to let myself be loved by her father for 1 extra, extra-long year.

A useless, endless year, if her father starts to hate me for not forgiving his daughter.

I have moments when I almost miss my loveless peace of mind. When I didn't question Circe's requisition of my 30-year-old unloved body-in-its-prime. Or the effectiveness of its sacrifice. Or the worthiness of her & my joint cause. Before Erinna's premature quartz threw a choice in my face, shocking me into an unaccustomed reality: of pain & of love.

My mother —& my father— had heard that someone had thrown a stone at me 1 moon ahead of time. Which they decided to interpret as an intervention of the gods on their behalf. For the benefit of their embarrassingly self-sacrificial daughter, who might perhaps be persuaded to commit suicide, now that she had tasted the experience of a first well-aimed stone.

Both my parents have always felt too enlightened to heed the promptings of the gods. Who according to my father lost their ubiquity to fixed temple images & to their written legends. & have faded away into subjective thought. Only slaves & uneducated workers still believe in them.

Not to mention their embarrassingly unenlightened daughter. Who had explained her sudden moonstruck ravings, after last year's Thargelia, as promptings from the moon goddess Circe. In whom their daughter suddenly claimed to believe, despite her obviously wasted education.

My parents have always agreed as parents, reserving their chronic disagreements for their conjugal relationship. When they heard about my molester, they instantly agreed wordlessly; just by looking at each other that I could always be trusted to choose the unexpected the socially least acceptable when given a choice. & might very well be trusted to add the embarrassment of publicly forgiving my molester to the ridicule & indecency of my public agony. With the selfishness of martyrs whose dedication to a cause completely blinds them to the feelings & needs of their close kin.

Which propelled my parents to take prompt unanimous action:

1) My mother would send me a message — Moving me with unexpected concern for my pains-to-come, & the offer of suicide.

2) My father would pay me a surprise visit, & talk to me about Socrates. Whose city-imposed death by hemlock had been documented step by step possibly embellished by his municipal attendant.

3) My mother would pay me a surprise visit 2 days later, & bring me the promised hemlock. For which I'd have been sufficiently prepared by then. At least enough not to refuse my mother's gift, but to take it & hide it in my bed —with Circe's supply of laurel leaves— in case I

experienced a return of reason, during a last-moment panic, that changed my sacrificial mind.

However, my parents had not counted on their embarrassing daughter to fall in love. With an uneducated man who disgracefully earned his living with his body.

Whose unexpected presence in my municipal room & bed completely jeopardized their unanimous plan. The lover of a common sponge diver no longer deserved to commit suicide, like the philosopher Socrates, almost painlessly, in dignified solitude. Deserving, on the contrary, to be stoned to death for the social disgrace she was inflicting upon her already sufficiently embarrassed parents . . .

At least this is how I try to explain to myself why my mother didn't bring me the hemlock she had offered. Why she didn't even mention her offer again.

Instead she commented on my bruised cheek. Which she took to be the handiwork of my uneducated lover.

To whom she had not linked my molester.

That was Erinna, the sponge diver's 12-year-old daughter, who had thrown the stone at me 1 moon ahead of time: I said, pointing to the back of the eye-exercising girl.

& this was my mother: I said to Erinna.

Who instantly stopped exercising. & turned around, placing her palms over her eyes, as she has been instructed to do at the end of each exercise. Conveniently avoiding my mother's contemptuous scrutiny.

What would she do if she were inadvertently given the power of life or death over a 12-year-old motherless girl
who was her lover's daughter   at the cost of 1 year of life to herself? I whispered in my mother's ear.

She recoiled at the words 'her lover's' as though Circe had changed me into a hissing snake. But quickly reinclined her mouth in my direction, advising me to reread our classic tragedies. Which were filled with conflicts of this nature. Although they were royal conflicts, & if a character appeared in the guise of a fisherman, he usually was a god, or at least a noble hero, travelling incognito: she sighed. Rising to her feet. Almost running from the room.

Erinna promptly uncovered her eyes, looking questions at me. Yes: I said to her: That was my mother.

Solar theologies belittle the moon. They discredit it as the dark power that brought death to man, who had previously lived eternal, shedding old age like a moulting snake.
Yet, they look to the same dark power's faculty of renewal
   —the moon dies every month & resurrects after 3 days—
to grant eternal life.
—The alternative of which is sexual intercourse: The parents surviving in the child, grandchild, etc., ad infinitum-holocaustum.—

Herbs gathered by the light of the moon are said to restore youth.

Initially the moon was androgynous: Luna & Lunus.
The male side was 'the keeper of the seed of the bull' (semen: the moon controls all that is liquid) to whose 'spirit of vengeance' the warriors of ancient Greece pledged themselves before going to battle.
The male moon allegedly impregnated (the) women (of Thebes), who conceived male children during its waxing, & female children during its waning phase.

It also impregnated hares, 1 of 3 lunar animals. All hares were thought of as females, procreating exclusively through the agency of the male side of the androgynous moon.

The female side of the androgynous moon was associated with the female elements:
WATER (blood/semen/sap). —Baptism is a vestige from moon-worship times.
& EARTH —through plants & wood. Lunar deities were sometimes worshipped as trees, or as living inside trees, whose sap rises & falls according to the phases of the moon.

The female elements water & earth are: static & lasting; horizontal; dark.
The male elements fire & air are: mobile & passing; vertical; light.

& with WOMEN, who initially had exclusive control of water & wood. Drawing water (making rain), the gathering of fire wood, & maintaining the sacred flame —(the male element: fire depends on the female element: wood to which it clings for its existence, devouring it in the process)— in the shrines of Demeter (who execrated marriage), Kore, Aphrodite (Venus), & Pan were the sacred duties of women.
If a man entered these holy shrines, he lost his shadow — linked to female darkness; often considered the seat of the soul—. Unauthorized animals lost their fertility.
(Hecate, the goddess of the underworld, was associated with the dark —female— side of the moon.)

Initially all women were thought to possess the gift of prophecy. When they drank moon wine, or chewed ivy or

laurel leaves, the moon entered their bodies, through whose agency it communicated future events.
—Before worried men began to blame women & the moon for man's fall, & the origin of death, & began to burn prophetic women as witches.—

At the beginning of agriculture, which introduced a fixed (horizontal) life style & (vertical) hierarchy, the moon began to be addressed as a female deity
—perhaps preserving the 2 androgynous sides grammatically by making the total a feminine entity. Certain French words —*amour, delice,* & *orgue*/love, delight, & (musical) organ— which are masculine in the singular become feminine in the plural—
& men feared that, if the lunar power was worshipped as a goddess, wives would be absolute masters of husbands.

But whether male, female, or both, the moon has always been the measure of time. —It takes 9 lunations to produce a human life. 9 is the number of completion; & of water.— The 'apportioner', whom Sophocles equals to destiny. The 3 Moirai or 3 Fates are the 3 phases of the moon. As were Faith, Hope, & Charity, the 3 daughters of Holy Sophia (Wisdom), who was initially the moon.
(Metis, the goddess of Wisdom, shares the root of her name with the Moon.)
The number of the moon is 30, rounded up from the 29 days, 12 hours, 44 minutes, & 2.8 seconds it takes to complete its monthly cycle. Which is divided into 2 small black parts, & 1 large white one.
—Aristotle reports that the serpent has as many ribs as there are days in the lunar month.—

Lunar deities are commonly tri-une. & there are 3 lunar

animals: The DOG —on the XVIIIth trump card of the Tarot, 2 dogs bay at the moon. The card signifies: Strangeness error deception, including self-deception hidden enemies.

The CAT —which allegedly grows fat when the moon waxes, & lean when it wanes. & its eyes widen or narrow accordingly. (It still rains cats & dogs.)

& the HARE —which was sacred to Dionysus (Bacchus), a moon god who sometimes changed into a hare, & to Artemis (Diana), a moon goddess sometimes depicted as a hare.
Eating hare's flesh was said to make women attractive & fertile (pregnancy test).
An ointment made of hare's fat brought out the witch nature in a woman. & if a hare crossed one's path, especially from right to left, it was a bad omen.
The hare's symbolic reputation continues alive in the Easter Bunny. & Easter itself is a moon-dependent holiday, celebrated on the first Sunday after the full moon that falls on or follows March 21.
(Eostre, the Celtic goddess of Dawn —Greek: Eos; Roman: Aurora— stood for the coming of spring, & for fertility. Her symbols were: the rabbit/the egg/the lily.)

Although not an official lunar animal, the SERPENT also belongs to the moon, because of its faculty of moulting renewal.
Asklepius, the god of healing, was initially a moon god in serpent form, at a time when healing was still done mainly by women, before the moon lost its androgyny & became a female deity.

To this day the caduceus, 1 or 2 serpents twined about a staff, is the symbol of medicine.

All stones partake of the lunar nature, because they are considered to be everlasting & indestructible. Especially hard crystalline gems which seem to emit light, a virtue they owe to the moon.
The moonstone, a translucent feldspar with pearly luster, is the philosopher's stone which transforms base metals (& souls) into gold.
—With the aid of an otherwise undying serpent with one diamond eye.—
Teeth were also primitively associated with the moon, because they were optimistically thought of as everlasting.
—Dreaming of losing teeth is interpreted as a warning of someone's death.—

The moon was said to stimulate the growth of hair, which some considered to be 'the seat of the soul'. According to others the soul lived in the liver, the intestines, or in a person's shadow.

Plutarch says: The effects of the moon are similar to the effects of reason & wisdom (Artemis & Dionysus), whereas those of the sun appear to be brought about by the power of physical force & violence (Apollo).

Solar gods are later gods, & their attributes are taken from the lunar deities that preceded them. In primitive thought the sun had no significance at all. At most, it was thought of as the consort of the male side of the androgynous moon. (In Germanic languages the moon is masculine, the sun feminine.)

29th & last day of Mounichion

Watching Erinna orbit around her father, who orbits around me —or rather: around the immortal moon goddess & seductress Circe, ever more firmly established inside me— reminds me of myself, at 12, going on 13. When I, too, had showered exaggerated demonstrations of affection alternatingly upon my father & whoever happened to be the object of my father's attention at the time. Bouncing from my father to the object to my father in a clumsily erratic dance, like a firefly signalling its need for love. Hoping to make the object jealous by soliciting similar demonstrations from my father. With the graceless bluntness of my age.

Doubtlessly provoking the gesture my father made, one languid summer afternoon in his teaching room, in front of his then-current student-object. Whose eyes widened appreciably when my father interrupted his lecture on power politics to cup my 12-to-13-year-old breasts in his languid summer hands & whisper in my ear that: They were growing rounder every day.
Making it sound like a promise.
Which plunged my 12-to-13-year-old conscience into a loyalty conflict in my relationship with my mother. To whom I felt I owed a report of what my father had done, & said. But I didn't want to spoil the promise of increased paternal affection —especially of paternal attention— which I thought I had heard in his whisper voice, nor my first triumph over one of his student-objects, by provoking a dinner attack from my mother.
Finally I told my nurse. Who told me: Not to tell my mother anything. To forget about it. Fathers were men, too, & the gestures men made, & the things men said were

meant for when they made & said them, but seldom meant the same thing   anything   afterwards.

Men lived in the present: my nurse said to me: But for women the present contained the future. Like the chicken containing the egg, at the beginning of chickens. & as women gave birth to the future, their present contained also the past. Which was why women looked for continuity where men looked for change.

Time was the conflict between men & women. Which men measured by the sun, & women by the moon.

Which needn't be a conflict, if men & women realized that continuity cannot exist except in change. But few couples reached that understanding between themselves. As immortally demonstrated by the conjugal battles of Zeus & Hera.

My nurse was not ordinarily given to lengthy explanations, & what she said made sense to me. It seemed to explain the dinner deadlock between my parents.

I had almost forgotten about the whole afternoon when my mother opened that evening's dinner conversation with the pointed question: What my father thought he was teaching me   or his witnessing students   by making sexual overtures to his adolescent daughter. Fathers seducing their daughters   my mother believed   was a taboo even among the most promiscuous of classical heroes. & even our gods' love of family didn't go beyond marrying their sister, to my mother's knowledge. But of course my mother had not had my father's privileged access to higher learning.

My father looked lightning bolts at me, which turned me the color of shame.

Which is also the color of rage.

Which began to boil inside me as I continued to sit dumbly between my parents, the continued subject of their dinner battle, but ignored. A hole in the ground, into which they dumped their irritation with each other.

Incest was the least of his temptations: my father replied, in a voice of ice. Not on moral grounds so much as on the ground of family-arity. Which was proverbially known for breeding contempt. He would have to be very hard up indeed before he'd think of saying or doing whatever my adolescent wishdreams had denounced him for having said. Or done. To my mother. Deviously feeding my mother's chronic jealousy to feed my adolescent self-importance. Pitting my parents against each other in clumsy childish misinterpretation of his recent lecture on power politics: Divide in order to rule. My devious manipulations augured well for the kind of woman my mother's daughter was growing up to be. He pitied the man who . . . etc . . .

I wrote my first poem that evening   another full-moon evening   by the light of the moon. It was called: Hate Freeze. Or: Hate Frieze. I no longer remember which, but I remember that I was ferocious in my hurt.

Spilling my rage:

Against my father. Who was making me feel like an undesirable lump, after having made me feel desirable for the first time in my life, earlier that afternoon.

Making me wonder if I had imagined what my father had said & done to me. Which   as my nurse had said   had had no meaning, even if I had not imagined what he had done & said. In front of the then-current student-object. Whose widening eyes I had perhaps also imagined.

& against my nurse. Who had betrayed me. After setting me up. Doing the very thing she had cautioned me not to do: Tell my mother.

& most of all   against my mother. Who had used me

as a club in her dinnertime warfare with my father. Creating
the false impression that I had told on my father.
Without thinking how this must affect his feelings for me.

Or worse: perhaps thinking precisely that. Making sure
that my father no longer trusted me. Or even liked me.
That I, at least, would never be her rival.

Which was what happened. & changed my relationship
with both my parents from the affection-seeking teenage
daughter to a boarder. Whose sole intimacy was with the
written word. It created what my mother called: 'My
willful isolation', in her carefully humorous message to
me.

I think of that year when I was 12, going on 13 as a
plateau of awareness in my life. When I felt that I knew all
there was to know about human relationships. At least in
theory.

Human relationships I thought then could all be
reduced to: Manipulator & Manipulated. With an
occasional switch of roles, due to a rebellion on the part of
the manipulated.

The officially manipulated slaves, like my nurse got
even through betrayal. Which they cultivated like an art.
Chuckling as they sowed distrust & dislike among their
masters. Who had been stupid enough to confide in them.

& the unofficially manipulated married women, like
my mother tried to get even through blame. Which
they expressed through relentless nagging. Which created
lies/betrayal on the part of the denying blamed manipulator. & ill humor: nagging my increasingly ill-humored
father to seek his satisfactions farther & farther away from
her.

It was not a happy year. Nor were the next 17 to 18 years

which I continued to live in my parents' house, rarely speaking to either of them. & never again speaking to my nurse. Although she begged to speak with me almost daily. Humbly, & red-eyed from weeping.

Her death, 2 years ago, overwhelmed me with guilt when I found out from another old slave woman that my nurse, who had understood the reason for my sudden silence, had desperately wanted me to know: that it had not been she, but the student-object with the widened eyes, who had informed my mother of my father's languid summer gesture.

I have no memory of a specific event, happy or unhappy, that might have refuted or borne out my theories about human relationships. Yet, I'd been considerably better off than my lover's daughter. At least I'd not needed to beg forgiveness of any of the many objects of my father's wandering attention — not even of my blaming, blameless mother— in the hopes of saving my 12-year-long life. As Erinna is hoping to do, with her touchingly blatant attempts (which *her* father does not call: her devious manipulations) to be included in her father's affection for me. Hoping to force me to forgive her at least in private, which is a trap to force me to forgive her also in public through my love of her father's love for me.

One such blatantly touching attempt —devious manipulation— is a poem: 'Stones Don't Want To Be Thrown', with which she surprised me this afternoon.

> My quartz decries the hand
> that cut your cheek
> and with it cut
> the thread of that hand's life.

Forgive the selfish hand
my father loves
almost as much
as he loves your bruis'd cheek.

Forgive the blameless quartz
which cut your cheek
against its will.
Stones wish to heal, not hurt.

Repentant and ashamed
I hold my quartz
as it refracts
the pale tears of the moon.

It is a surprising first poem coming from a 12-year-old sponge diver's daughter who has just learned to form the letters of the alphabet. To translate these unaccustomed visual symbols back into accustomed sounds.

It probably is a better poem than my Hate Frieze or Freeze. My primal scream of betrayed trust, & loveless undesirability. I'm amazed how fast & well Erinna learns. Perhaps because her mind is fresh, unspoiled by education. By teachers who place themselves on pedestals, forcing their students to look up to them. Tilting their students' eyes to the impressionable 120-degree angle of worship. Which is the angle of our mental screen. On to which the gods project the visions of blind seers. & of believers who pray to them with their eyes closed. But which opens a hypnotic chute to the mind when the eyes are open. As students' eyes are supposed to be. Making their minds defenselessly impregnable. Adoringly ready to absorb the teacher's teachings. Along with the teacher's prejudices/-frustrations/pedantry.

My primal scream of hate what I remember of it now,

close to 18 years & hundreds of poems later; mainly its
stilted self-serious bitterness   probably echoed the loveless
love forays of my self-serious father. Whose prescriptions
of laughter were meant for others. For his blameless blaming wife, & his undesirable-feeling lump of a daughter.

Erinna's poem echoes no one. It is an original outcry
of threatened 12-year-old flesh. Of a 12-year-old mind,
drastically ripened by the prospect of death.

Which is only 6 days away. For her, if not for me. For
me, if not for her.

I've been imagining irrefutable arguments that would
persuade my parents to supply a sponge diver's sweetheart
with hemlock.   —Which would preclude forgiving
Erinna, & leave her stuck with my sacrifice.

& I've rehearsed sentences that would compel my conscientious attendant to take Erinna & me on an evening
stroll to the distant harbor. As step One in my lover's
escape plan for Erinna & me together. Which is doomed
to fail.

& I've envisioned passing by my ever-vigilant attendant
at the door, disguised as: my lover/my father/my attendant.

& I've implored Circe to change me into a bird.

& I see no way out.

Stones of varying sizes representing the basic female shape
are the earliest symbols of worship in existence. Stones
belong to the moon-ruled female element earth, & are
feminine in the same   mostly romance   languages that
speak of the moon as SHE, & of the sun as HE. Accordingly
stones are thought of as: static—lasting/life-conserving/
healing.
Early healers frequently used stones to relieve stomach-

related ailments. —Astrology associates the stomach with the zodiac sign Cancer, a cardinal water sign which is ruled by the moon. The earth is said to have taken its shape during the Cancerian age, & become inhabited by dinosaurs, etc.—

Flat black river stones applied to painful areas of the lower back were believed to draw out & absorb kidney & bladder disorders. Sometimes the stones were boiled, & patients drank the water, which allegedly dissolved kidney stones, & cured cystitis.
For menstrual cramps, porous rust-colored stones were warmed & placed on the lower abdomen or the small of the back.
Jade especially pale green or white jade was worn in China as a protection against infectious diseases, skin allergies, & epilepsy. Rich Chinese ate powdered jade to cure acidity of the stomach & stiffness of the joints.
A moonstone worn on the left index finger protected the sanity of medieval alchemists, & made them impervious to the enticement of invoked demons.

As late as the 17th century AD the historically constipated Cardinal de Richelieu (1585–1642) is said to have swallowed a small black pebble the size & shape of a kidney bean* —possibly a bean-shaped piece of lead— every

*bean: Pythagoras,** the Samos-born philosopher, mathematician, & religious reformer (582–500 BC), who taught the doctrine of sexual equality, did not permit his students to practice sacrifice, kill harmless animals, chop down trees, or eat flesh, eggs, or beans. The bean was considered an unholy, lascivious food, & not eating beans encouraged chastity.

**Pythagoras married one of his students when he was 60, & had 7 children.

night upon going to bed, which was believed to encourage a bowel movement in the morning. Although the prudent cardinal allegedly also had recourse to a daily enema. Which was administered to him in the morning before he held his audiences or went to people's houses for political discussions. Allegedly he had his commode carried into the conference room or else requested a commode from his hosts, in whose salon the meeting was held. Over which he allegedly presided, enthroned upon the commode. From which allegedly rose an olfactory argument that refuted all possible opposition.

Thargelion 1

Erinna has been cross-eyed all day. She's having her first period, & panicked, waking up in a puddle of blood. Which she mistook for preparatory punishment, insidiously inflicted by our attendant during her sleep.

She expected perhaps she still expects the conscientious man to return to her cot during the remaining 5 nights, to wound her in other areas, until her body becomes one large bleeding wound, into which all the men of Athens will throw their stones on Expulsion Day.

I attributed her gory fantasy to her nurseless upbringing, & tried to dispell it, patiently explaining the cyclic cleansing of women's bodies. & the moon's control of our cycles, comparing it to the tides of the ocean, with which she seems to have a more intimate relationship than with her body. Thinking that I was reassuring her about her sudden womanhood by giving it a place in the cosmic order.

But her left pupil fled to the nose corner of the eye & disappeared completely as she refused to be reassured.

Staring at me   or past me   in furrow-browed distrust. As
though she suspected me of being in league with our
attendant. Hissing: When was I finally going to do what
her father has been asking me to do?

She knows about her father's plan for our escape.
Unfortunately. & has been whispering to me about it.
Asking: When . . . ? Sometimes in the presence of our
attendant. Feeding his civil-servant's distrust of sponge
divers & other common fishing folk who earn their scanty
living independently, without the security of official
servitude. Nudging me, when he brings our meals, to ask
him to take us on a stroll to the water.

Her father's plan is not as easy to carry out as he insists
it is. With growing impatience. & with the confidence of
a man used to adapting his body to the hazardous demands
of the moment. A confidence which also underestimates
the intelligence of civil servants.

He shrugs instantly mimicked by his daughter when
I point out that: A leisurely stroll to the harbor is too far a
walk to request without arousing the instant suspicion of
our attendant. The man is not stupid. & his professional
vigilance has been personalized by jealousy. Further sharp-
ened by Erinna's recent whispering. He'd instantly guess
that my sponge-diver lover was behind my unreasonable
request. & pity me, thinking like my mother that the
sponge diver had become my lover only to dupe me into
helping him steal his daughter & obstruct municipal
justice.

Which would sadden him, at the realization of my
gullibility & misplaced trust.

& gladden him, because it will show me the sponge diver
& his daughter for what they really are. After he spoils
their plan.

—Which he prepares to spoil, as he smilingly agrees to take us on our walk. To teach me my lesson.

Erinna grins triumphantly. Further confirming his suspicion. Which has been tirelessly active since Mounichion 19, when he reported her father's unexplained early-morning presence in our municipal bridal chamber to the authorities. While pretending to accept my explanation: That I wished to acquire 3 large sponges for my baths.

Which the conscientious civil servant used to enjoy preparing & administering to me, the first Thargelia bride in his municipal care & experience who is neither deformed, nor disease-ridden, nor otherwise repulsive.

But has enjoyed preparing & administering to me much less since Erinna's incorrigible insistence on helping him with his womanly chores.

Since Mounichion 21, other civil servants disguised as athletes have been trailing us on our walks.

They are trailing us again on our stroll to the water's edge, disguised as discus throwers — *diskoboloi* — on their way to practice along the strand. Anticipating the gagging & binding of my attendant by Erinna's father & his friends.

—To which I object anyway: I'm loath to deceive the conscientious man & become the first flaw on his flawless record. I'm not their hero Ulysses. —

The *diskoboloi* allow Erinna's father & his friends to gag & bind our attendant just long enough to establish the evidence of her father's abduction scheme. —Her abduction, not mine. — Which will condemn us all.

We would have a better chance following my initially teasing, playful suggestion that: Her father & I trade roles. That he bring a sponge diver's outfit for me, the next time he comes to visit & eat supper with us.

Which he has been eating with us regularly since Mouni-chion 26, the evening after my father's surprise visit. My attendant no longer asks: If we'll be three for supper. He formally carries in a third meal, & withdraws.

I suggest that I change into my lover's clothes after our next supper. & walk from the room. Past my attendant at the outer door. Down the long municipal hall, with its columns shaped like gigantic mushrooms. Down the 14 municipal steps. & out . . .

After we make love, after supper. After Erinna goes to sleep, or pretends to go to sleep, her jealous little face turned to the wall.

Which may be the last time we may be sure of making love, our passion heightened by our fear that we may really be making love for the last time if my escape plan fails.

If I fail to walk unrecognized past my ever-vigilant attendant, in my sponge diver's disguise. If he recognizes & questions my womanly fullness under the clinging top.

While my lover stays behind, pretending to be me, asleep. Dealing with my attendant through Erinna having Erinna whisper: That I was exhausted from the still throbbing pain in my cheek. That I've finally fallen asleep. In case my attendant came in. For whatever reason. To check up on us after he has seen the sponge diver leave. & suddenly has a strange feeling about how the sponge diver looked, or walked, from the back, on his way out.

My lover will wait until the hour before daybreak the darkest hour, when Athenians hold their funeral celebrations. When he'll change back into a sponge diver; into the second sponge-diver suit he brought, & once again

scale the municipal wall in the opposite direction: down
with Erinna slung across his shoulder.

Which had, after all, been his own initial plan. On
Mounichion 19. A plan which had almost succeeded.
Which had failed only because Erinna had awakened me
with her pre-dawn whispering.

Just as my plan might fail only after I've successfully
walked past my attendant. Who has not recognized me,
despite my womanly fullness. But who recognizes my walk
down the long column-lined municipal hall, from the back.
Which I relaxed, & stopped watching, as I reached the top
of the 14 municipal steps.

Or it might fail if I lose my way, & cannot find the spot
where my lover & Erinna are to join me. On my lover's
friend's fishing boat.

& might still fail if we all find each other at the spot at
the harbor, but his friend & his fishing boat fail to be there.

His friend has been sitting in his boat, waiting, in
readiness, losing out on catching fish, for the last 4 nights:
my lover says, bitter-lipped, reproachful.

My dramatization of the pitfalls of his plan, & of my
equally unrealistic counter-proposal convince neither my
lover nor his echo of a daughter.

Who is sitting up on her cot, staring at or past me, cross-
eyed with distrust & open hostility. Keeping herself awake.
I don't know if she's waiting for the nightly appearance of
her father who is unusually late; we finally ate supper
without him or if she's still expecting an insidious punitive
visit from our attendant.

Who may be responsible for my lover's unusual lateness. & may have found a way to prevent further visits from my lover. Whose unexplained first pre-dawn visit he has belatedly reported to the city fathers. Who are prohibiting further visits from my lover, because my attendant has informed them of his suspicion that the sponge diver had come to steal his daughter, on Mounichion 19. Which I had prevented, that first time, but might no longer be able to prevent, because . . . Etc.

I, too, am sitting up in bed. Worrying about what may be delaying my lover. Thinking up & discarding plans of escape. Wondering if my mother might still be persuaded to bring me the hemlock she had offered. But then never mentioned again during her visit, after the public embarrassment of my shabby self-sacrifice was blotted from her mind by the still shabbier embarrassment of my having taken an uneducated sponge diver for a lover.

Who still has not come.

With whom I trade places, dreamily, reclining on my bed:
He comes in, dressed as the traditional Thargelia transvestite, a necklace of pale-green figs around his salt-cured neck. He starts walking down the columned hall, & down the 14 municipal steps. He stops on the 11th step &, grandly gesturing to my attendant, publicly forgives Erinna.

— Who has fallen asleep in her sitting position, her head angled against the wall beside her cot. —

Dressed as a sponge diver I take Erinna by the hand, to

pull her through the thickening crowds, in the direction of the shore. Where we disappear among the common fishing folk, who agree to take us to Circe's island of Aeaea for the price of the moonstone on my left index finger.

But Erinna wants to stay. & add her quartz to the stones of the others. To my white marble ball, & miniature full moon the size of a child's head, which I aim at my lover's temple to drive out his worshipful emulation of Ulysses.

—Who had also kept women waiting. Who'd kept Penelope waiting for 20 years. —

& prove that women, too, can live by their wits. Namely: Let others die so that they can go on living.

By the 3rd century BC women's moon-ruled menstrual cycle had been decreed unclean. Which made women unfit for conducting religious rites. At best it restricted their participation in religious rites to women over 60. — Apollo's priestesses were post-menopausal virgins.—

With the exception of funeral rites,* which continued to be celebrated by women of all ages. Although here, too, women over 60 were eventually preferred.

By the 3rd century BC the presence of menstruating women was thought to:

> turn new wine sour
> wither the crops
> make grafts drop off

*In Athens, funerals were held during the hour immediately preceding daybreak. The mouth of the corpse was tied or sewn up & the body was placed in a grave facing west. Mourners wore black, & sometimes partially sheared their heads. Men in mourning were allowed to wear women's clothes.

kill bees
dry up seeds
make unripe fruit fall from trees
dull metals
dim mirrors
rust iron & bronze
poison the air
turn freshly washed linen black

If a dog tasted of menstrual blood, it went mad & its bite became deadly, as with rabies.

Menstrual blood placed in a vessel outside attracted lightning, & drove the storm away.

Thargelion 2

I had given up waiting, & was floating on the pale-blue plain of early sleep when my lover walked in last night. Less lithe on his feet than usual. He collapsed against me on the bed, breathing hard. I smelled the wine he'd been drinking without me as he lay shaking in my arms, salting my skin with his tears. Crying: That he could no longer endure the tension of my indecision. Which was sure to cost him the passion of his life, if not the life of his daughter.

& was making him impotent.

Threatening to stay away & not see or touch me any more for the miserly 3 days of love life we have left, unless I promised not to wait another day, to ask the attendant to walk Erinna & me to the harbor as soon as we'd been served our next midday meal.

Which I promised to do. Against my better judgment. I know the attendant will instantly become suspicious, &

refuse. Or rather: He'll pretend that he hasn't heard me. Which is how he has always handled my requests to have Erinna sent home.

I've told my lover that we'd have a better chance if I just asked the attendant to take us for a walk, without saying where I want to go. If we just set out, & I then invoked the convincingly beautiful weather

—which has felt exceptionally beautiful to me this spring: As though nature were mirroring my first experience of love, making me want to postpone dying—

to stretch the walk. & lead us, as though inadvertently, to some convincingly scenic spot somewhere near the water. Where we would sit down to rest. & wait for my lover to find us, to take us aboard his friend's fishing boat.

But my lover insists that: We need to be directly across from the spot where the boat sits waiting —has been sitting in waiting readiness for a full week, losing catches of fish— to be whisked aboard before any unprogrammatic resistance on my attendant's part attracts a commotion.

& so I sighed. & promised. & let my reason drown in his desperate desire.

Which lasted all night. He made up for his unusually late arrival by staying with me until the room became filled with the same undecided half-light in which I had first caught sight of him bending over Erinna's cot on bowed bare legs when Erinna had awakened me with her whispering.

Without Erinna's whispering my lover would have remained the unseen father of my cross-eyed 12-year-old molester. One of many anonymous sponge divers, whose worship of Ulysses & disregard for the moon goddess Circe had annoyed me when I'd heard it echoed from the lips of his daughter.

—Whom he had somehow managed to carry from the room, with the complicity of my undisturbed sleep. Miraculously eluding my attendant's conscientious vigilance.—

& I would have remained an unloved 30-year-old virgin. Who would be going to her shabby martyr's death 3 days from now, without having known the experience of fulfilled desire. Compensating with martyrdom for passions she never tasted.

Who would have sat out her Thargelia-bride lifespan chewing laurel leaves. Trying to convert fear-mirages of pains to come —sewn into her still-throbbing left cheek by the premature quartz of her 12-year-old cross-eyed molester—

back into the rainbow ecstasy of dying for a worthy cause.

About which I've resumed arguing with the moon goddess Circe inside my head.

I'm nervous, & full of doubt. Afraid that my voice will betray my anxiety to the attendant when I make my unreasonable request this afternoon. Against my better judgment. The man has heard me only calm-voiced & composed. Even the morning after the incident with Erinna's quartz, when I persuaded him with bleeding cheek not to keep my cross-eyed molester chained to the wall by her ankles.

Before my cheek became swollen & infected, & I learned the reality of pain, devoid of ecstasy.

I've been plagued with fear-mirages all morning, in anticipation of asking my attendant.

My limp body lies in disarray a crumple of rags outside the city gates. Too exhausted finally to go on breathing.

My stone-bruised eyelids close on the repulsive sight of my agonizing groom. Who is the last sight I see on this earth. Who chokes my last breath with the stench of his fear as he crumples on top of me.

Or: I'm still far from the city gates. I've stumbled & fallen many times. My bridal dress is torn in many places, exposing bruised intimate flesh. A sticky juice is leaking from the figs around my neck. Mixing with the blood leaking from many wounds. The sticky mixture has attracted flies, which sting my face, my arms, my stone-bruised eyelids.

I lie bruised & exhausted, my swollen eyes staring up at my embarrassed father. Who bows with mock gallantry as he prods me back on my feet, striking me painfully across my exposed pudenda with a willow rod budding with silky catkins.

I fall again, & lie staring up at my embarrassed mother. Who walks away, stepping on my hands.

Again I'm painfully prodded to my feet. This time by Erinna, who sticks her tongue out at me as she inserts her quartz into my left eye socket.

Again I crumple, & lie staring up at my lover. Whose face wrinkles in disgust at the spectacle of my shameless shame.

All of which may or may not happen. But whatever happens, I must go through with it, for the sake of women & the moon. Whom I cannot betray at the last moment, sneaking out with the lover she so providentially found for me: Circe carries on inside my head.

Besides, whatever happens will cause me neither pain, nor shame, nor even embarrassment. But will glide past on the periphery of my perception like someone else's dream, as long as I keep chewing laurel leaves.

Which I stopped chewing after the sponge diver became my lover. In case the chewing numbs also the sensation of desire. & of its fulfilment. Which I want to experience with keen senses.

Which I may be experiencing for the last time early this afternoon, when my lover comes to visit immediately after our midday meal. He wants to be present when I ask my attendant to walk Erinna & me to the harbor.
— After we make love. For the one more time we can be sure to make love. While Erinna rolls her eyes before the exercise chart I drew for her on the wall above the black ankle hooks, 6 times to the right, & 6 times to the left, her turned bony back brittle with jealousy. Or while she practices the alphabet, frowning down on her letters, watching us from under lowered lids.

Erinna's presence in the room neither inhibits nor heightens my passion. Which makes me forget that she's there. But my lover feels inhibited. —He isn't even sure he wants to or can make love this last time, early this afternoon.— He doesn't want his daughter to start thinking that she's undesirable, because sitting in on our passion is making her feel left out.
My uneducated lover is more sensitive to the feelings of his 12-year-old daughter than my learned father was to mine. Which my father seemed to hurt wilfully, some- times, when I was 12 years old, going on 13, when he seemed to derive added satisfaction from playing his seduction games in front of me. Pointedly excluding me from his affection even from his attention after the denunciation of his languid summer gesture by the witness- ing wide-eyed student-object.
Who had also felt excluded.

As has my attendant. Who will feel further excluded perhaps offended when my lover attempts to fool his suspicion by shocking him. With total insensitivity for the feelings of a civil servant.

My lover plans to remain stretched out on my bed while I ask my attendant to take Erinna & me on our escape walk to the harbor. & before the conscientious man can say either yes or no, my lover will declare: That he'll be waiting for us 'right here'. That I've worn him out. Draining all his energy, which is now inside me. Making me eager to go on a long walk, while he can barely take another step. He'll take a nap on my bed until Erinna & I come back. Around supper time. . .

Which I find in poor taste. But which made Erinna laugh.

2 more hours, & I will have kept my unreasonable promise & made my unreasonable request.

2 more days & 14 hours   —after my attendant refuses to be fooled—   & I will have made the decision that will save or condemn Erinna. Or me.

Which I will have made even if I decide nothing.

When I will have decided to continue anticipating my scheduled death for 384 more days. In the conscientious care of my joyfully unfooled attendant. While my cheek gradually heals. & my lover's love for me turns into hate, after the stoning to death of his 12-year-old cross-eyed daughter.

Whom I cannot possibly condemn. To whom I owe the experience of my love as much as my fear-mirages of pains to come.

Whom I must therefore decide to forgive. Before a

crowd of incredulous Athenians. Perhaps including my embarrassed parents.

My lover will not believe my decision. Or he'll believe it, but the prospect of my death will affect him as if I decide nothing. i.e. as if I decide his daughter's death. & he'll stay away for the miserly 2 days & 14 hours of our remaining love life, declaring that the continued anticipation of death be it mine or his daughter's is making him impotent.

Which contradicts the theory that the proximity of death prompts sexual desire. As evidenced by skeletons linked in coitus positions found in the ruins of besieged palaces, or whole cities. Skeletons of persons who had experienced a death similar to the one Circe continues to urge upon me. An anticipated death, that does not take by surprise. That slowly steps from the shadows of the future, defining itself ever more sharply with each waiting day.

Which looks extremely sharp, from my 2-day-&-13¾-hour perspective.

& may have been what prompted me, 10 days & 10¼ hours ago, to let the sponge diver *a* sponge diver reach for me, on my Thargelia-bridal bed, that first tingling Mounichion afternoon. While his daughter Erinna exercised her eyes, which she covered with her palms after the exercise, peeking at her father & me through her fingers.

Which I might not have let happen in full view of a normal life expectancy spreading before me. Under normal circumstances. In my wilfully isolated boarder's room in my parents' house, for instance.

Which would have been considered highly abnormal.

By my parents & all of Athens, including other sponge
divers & common fishing folk. Who have all been indoctri-
nated with the 'new man's' way of thinking. & of writing.
& re-writing. Which obliterates or at least discredits
(moon) goddesses & princesses, & poetesses of earlier
times who had often taken lovers who were their social
inferiors. Even slaves.

& would the sponge diver have reached for me, if the
proximity of death had not overruled his 'new man's'
considerations of propriety —which have trickled down
the social ladder & have reached the common folk— if he
had not been prompted by the scheduled proximity of his
daughter's death? Which he knew or believed to be 12
days & 13¾ hours away. & which affected him like his
own.

& became the ulterior motive for becoming my lover
—promptly overruled by genuine lust. Which the grateful flesh promptly converted into love—
at which my mother hinted, during her announced
surprise visit. In retaliation for humiliating my father.
Who humiliated my mother during every dinner conversation I was old enough to sit in on. But by whose
humiliation my mother claims to feel humiliated also.

& as my punishment for having taken a lover. & for
being happy for the first time in my 30-year-long life.
Which my mother has risked neither to do, nor to be.

2 days & 13½ hours.
Circe insists that mortals fear death because it is the one
act of nature man has learned to duplicate. Which prevents
him from seeing the positive side —the release from
concern & responsibility for earthly future; from which an
immortal goddess of the moon can never be released—

& concentrates his attention on the still life-connected act
of dying.

Medicine in ancient Greece

was originally practiced mostly by women, usually priestesses who allegedly kept tamed serpents in their temples.
Many of their many anonymous aphorisms about the
treatment of illnesses

> Healing requires love
> Every ailment has its natural antidote
> The natural world is an affront to man, & the treasure
>   trough of healers
> The more we nourish unhealthy bodies, the more we
>   injure them as we feed the illness
> Recommend abstinence, if the patient's strength can
>   sustain it
> Urine, the most reliable measure of health or disease
> In the treatment of arthritis, remember that it is often
>   caused by worry, or bereavement
> Wash your hands before & after treating each patient
> Use boiled water to clean out wounds
> Use boiled barley or lime water for purification
> For afflictions of eyes/ears/nostrils/breasts, treat both
>   even if only one is affected
> For infections of mouth/throat/genitals, be aware that
>   they are interrelated

were later attributed to the priest-physicians who succeeded them. (The 2 offices: of priest & of healer remained
inseparable for centuries.) Especially to Hippocrates

(approximately 460–377 BC) the best known of Greek physicians, who traveled widely in his attempts to combat malaria, 'the scourge of Greece', & is said to have practiced in Athens at the time of the Peloponnesian war (431–404 BC).

Hygiea, the Greek goddess of Health, another 'virgin' who used to be addressed as: 'Mother' Most High, eventually became known & worshipped mainly as the daughter of Asclepius (Roman Aesculapius; deified in the 8th century BC).

Art works often represent her as 'a maiden of kindly aspect', either at her father's side, or the most prominent among his attendants, offering milk to a serpent from a saucer.

In the Hippocratic oath, her name follows directly upon his. Asclepius is said to have received his instructions from the centaur Cheiron, who had a great knowledge of herbs, & the centaur image was engraved on rings worn by healers, & on healing rings which healers gave to patients to wear, as therapy.

(The herb Centaury mixed with Barberry leaves was used to cure jaundice in seventeenth-century England.)

Earliest methods of healing which survived for millennia:
    blood letting
    fumigation
    poulticing
    rubbing
    utrication —the application of nettles (utrica) to stimulate blood circulation
    stones —(heated) applied for stomach ailments, kidney & bladder disorders, menstrual cramps
    Precious stones worn on or near afflicted areas as therapy

Hypnotism
Clay images of afflicted areas/organs/limbs —ears,
  eyes, nose liver, kidneys, bladders hands, arms,
  feet offered to deities of healing.

Herbs, roots, & fruits played a major role in the treatment
of internal diseases, as fertility stimulants, prophylactics,
& to induce the healing of wounds or fractures. They were
usually gathered at night, according to specific phases of
the moon. The following is a selection of relatively familiar
names, & their uses:

Alfalfa	juice or powder, to prevent or cure arthritis.
Aloe	a cicatrizant.
Apple	whole apple cider vinegar is still used for gargling; & sub-sequently swallowed to cure soreness of throat. ½ cup taken daily to control blood-pressure & cure dizziness. A solution of ⅕ cider & ⅘ water to cleanse the female genitals.

(The 'lotus' of the Lotus Eaters in the *Odyssey* is
described as either a saffron-colored fruit, or as a fruit
resembling an apple. It allegedly produced loss of
memory, & was prescribed internally to cure
aggressiveness.)

Balsa modendron myrra (Myrrh)	to prevent miscarriages.
Belladonna	both a sedative & a heart stimu-lant; also a laxative.
Betony	to heal fractures of the skull.

Black hellebore	thought to cause diarrhoea upon mere touch. Its root was used as an emetic.
Borage	to cure ailments of the lungs.
Campanula (Rampion)	often eaten as a salad. It allegedly promotes fertility, in men as well as in women.
Chamomile	taken internally as a tea, to calm the heart. Externally to heal infections, especially conjunctivitis.
Colchicum	a carminative (expels gas from stomach).
Cyclamen	the root is chewed as an antidote against intoxication. The juice of the boiled root is used as a prophylactic.
Fig	the fruit: Internally to cure dysentery, externally to cure glandular swellings. The leaves: boiled, the water taken internally as a purifier.
Fraxinella	the flowers used for anesthesia.
Garlic	to control blood pressure.
Hemlock	a sedative in small doses; a lethal poison.
Iris	an emblem of mourning; a drink made from the boiled roots was used as a prophylactic.
Ivy	The leaves numb the senses when chewed; induce trance.
Kelp	contains vitamins A & E, & smaller percentages of B & D. It is a gentle purgative & bile

stimulant. It regulates the thyroid gland & prevents the formation of goiters. External application promotes the healing of broken bones, especially the brittle bones of older people.

Laurel
The leaves numb the senses when chewed; induce trance.

Leek
The juice, taken during pregnancy, prevents giving birth to monsters.

Mandrake
Monkshood }
Nightshade
powerful poisons, allegedly used by Hecate, Circe, & Medea.

Meadow Saffron
to relieve & cure gout.

Nettle
external application to cure palsy & paralysis. Rubbing the heart region with the leaves to stimulate blood circulation & revive persons in a coma.

Parsley
(worn as an emblem of mourning) Internally: an aphrodisiac; thought to promote good eyesight, especially night vision. The juice, taken during pregnancy, prevents giving birth to monsters.

Roses
Juice distilled from petals as an astringent. Used regularly to bathe the eyes prevents conjunctivitis.

Valerian
To calm the heart.

Thargelion 4

It took me a very long time to wake up this morning. Straining toward the surface of myself like a deep sea diver whose legs are entangled in algae.

—Which had happened to Erinna when she was not quite 8. When she'd tried to join her father underwater, at the bottom of the ocean: her father had told me. Admiringly: The not-quite-8-year-old Erinna had cut herself loose with a piece of coral. —

It was close to noon when I pushed my eyelids open. They felt like lead, in a head that felt like a large round stone. My body was wrapped in something hot & wet steaming linen & I was staring up into the intense gaze of a man whom I took to be my lover. Who was rubbing the region of my heart with nettles. Incidentally caressing my breasts with the backs of his hands at each circular motion.

He smiled at me, visibly relieved that his efforts were bringing me back to the surface. & I felt relieved, too, until I realized that I was staring up into the strangely smiling face of my attendant. Who instantly withdrew his hands from my breasts.

That I was being revived only to die a painful death. Which is scheduled to begin in 32 hours. & will mercifully be over with by the time of this writing 10 p.m. the day after tomorrow.

Which my lover may have wished to spare me when he laced my wine with hemlock juice —unwittingly fulfilling my mother's unkept promise— as we sat drinking in the municipal patio yesterday afternoon.

At the firmly polite suggestion of my attendant. Who responded to my unreasonable request: That he accompany Erinna & me on a walk to the harbor, on this unusually limpid spring day, exactly as I had expected him to respond: He pretended not to have heard me the first time. & when I repeated my request compelled by the locked stares of Erinna & my lover he suggested with irrefutable politeness that: We enjoy the unusual weather sitting on the benches of the municipal patio, with its spring-flowering shrubs, where we would be much more comfortable than on a long tiring walk through dusty city streets. Which we would, moreover, have to walk through again in darkness, on our way back.

Sparing himself the shock of my lover's stretching out on my bed. Declaring that: He'd be waiting for our return 'right here'. Followed by the implication that my sexual demands had exhausted him. Which I'd found in poor taste, when he'd told me what he intended to do. But which had made Erinna laugh.

Forcing us to rush outside to save face: after invoking the beauty of the weather instead of making at least the love my lover had been too nervous to make when he arrived earlier than he had said; Erinna & I were still eating our midday meal to be present when I made my unreasonable demand. Against my better judgment. To make sure I kept my promise.

I longed to make love all afternoon, & through the evening, & most of the night & again this morning/afternoon/evening/night every remaining moment of my irrevocably limited life. —While Erinna exercised her eyes, or practised the alphabet, or wrote another precocious poem. Or turned her jealous little face to the wall.

Inhibiting her father. Whose anticipation of losing the passion of his life —me— or perhaps his daughter, but not his own life was making him impotent.—

I sat in the municipal patio, flushed with desire. Counting: 62 more hours until I forgive Erinna . . . 61 more hours until I reach the city gates . . . Drinking the wine my lover kept pouring for me. & kept drinking with me, toasting: My merciful beauty, my beautiful mercy . . . to make sure I'd remember to forgive Erinna.

Who was blaming me for the attendant's refusal. Which I had predicted. Whisper-hissing that: I had waited too long to ask. That I had brought on the attendant's refusal by expecting it. Instead of trusting her father. . .

Who offered her a sip from his cup, to stop her whisper-hissing. She drank, but promptly spat it out. Making a face. Which made her father laugh. He hugged her, kissing her cheek. Telling her that: Wine was a grown-up taste, which she'd acquire soon enough if I gave her the chance to grow up. Toasting my beautiful . . . my merciful . . my poetic . . . my self-sacrificial. . .

Urging me to offer my attendant a drink also. From my cup. Which my attendant refused, with firm politeness. Smiling. Explaining that: Municipal employees were not permitted to drink while on duty.

Which: I smiled back: meant never, in his case, since he seemed to be on duty all the time.

He smiled more. I smiled more. My lover smiled. Erinna scowled. & I said that the first cup for drinking wine had been molded after the right breast of Helen of Troy.

I was hoping to rekindle my lover's anticipation-shrivelled desire by making him think of breasts. My breasts, which he loved to touch so much. Which he had said felt like the ocean on a warm summer night. I wanted him to want to stay. To share our supper, & afterwards my bed. But he shook his head, sadly, looking suddenly old. A haggard old man, who teetered slightly as he stood up to leave.

Erinna wrinkled her nose in disgust, & said prissily: She didn't understand why grown-ups liked to drink wine so much. Which tasted worse than salt water. Which tasted like resin. & only made people lose control over their legs.

I, too, seemed to be teetering when I stood up. Which surprised me: I had grown up drinking wine, in my parents' house. Sometimes I'd drunk up to 7 cups, writing poems through a night, in my isolated boarder's room.

I don't remember supper. Not what I ate, nor if I ate at all. I remember only that Erinna kissed me goodnight, unusually lovingly, after she renewed the aloe poultice I've been applying to the still-throbbing cut under my left eye. Which she brushed with her lips.

& I remember lying in my bed after supper, drowsily anticipating my lover's hands on my breasts. After he came back, probably late again, still drunker, from the despair of losing me. Or his daughter.

In whose place at the top of her cot, where her head used to lie, her jealous little face turned toward the wall he left a large sponge. After he did come back very late last night. & sober. Enough to sling his daughter over his shoulder & scale down the wall of the municipal building, while I slept my drugged sleep.

From which I wish I had not been awakened.

———————————————————————

During the 3rd century BC Athenians lived in flat-roofed houses, with patios in the back, covered with stone slabs.

They knew of glass, but did as yet not use it for windows or drinking vessels.

Their rooms were furnished with beds, chests, and broad individual stone seats that were attached to the walls.

Their entrances were guarded by porters, slaves bought for their stature, strength & beauty. —Beauty was of the greatest importance to Athenians.— Eventually the rich began to replace their live slave porters with imposing statues, and by the 3rd century BC, the fashion had trickled down to the households of physicians, philosophers & poets.

All housework was done by slaves, leaving the owners free to pursue their pleasures. They traveled widely, often on import/export business.

Exports from Athens included: wool linen cloth marbles jewelry engraved gems beds chests slippers books wine vinegar sweets fowl sheep anchovies quicksilver ochre cinnabar.

Money was lent at high interest, payable at the end of each month. But the city also had an extensive welfare system. Citizens paid regular amounts to a Benefit Club, a form of social security, as an insurance against sudden losses.

There were many public baths, free of charge. & doorless shelters, called Leschae, where anybody could spend the night. They were in great demand during wintertime, when the weather halted sponge & fishing trades, street vending, & other outdoor labors of the poor.

DEPOSITION

made on this the 4th Day of Thargelion before 5 of 6 assembled City Fathers. — The 6th City Father being detained in his home for reasons of health (gout). — And dictated to me, Lykaios, Official Record Maker and Record Keeper of the City of Athens, by one, Lithozelos, 1 of 2 Municipal Attendants assigned to Thargelia Volunteers, and other sacrificial bodies, either purchased or recruited and kept for emergency calamities.

CONCERNING: This year's Volunteer

Being exceptionally a female. And, moreover, neither deformed, nor diseased, nor a retired prostitute, nor a deficient slave. Not even properly destitute in the meaning commonly associated with that term. An alleged poetess, but nameless, without an audience, the 30-year-old unmarried, childless daughter of the philosopher Hippobotus, and of his wife Chlema. Accepted as this year's exceptional Voluntary Thargelia Bride by 1 of 6 City Fathers, whom she sought out in his home on the late evening of Last Thargelion 6, as per Thargelia Volunteer Application Form 2A, bearing her signature and that of the sought-out City Father. And unanimously confirmed by the 5 remaining City Fathers on the morning of Last Thargelion 7, as per additional Thargelia Volunteer Application Form 2B, bearing the signature of the 5 remaining City Fathers, in addition to those of the first City Father and the Volunteer. And

CONCERNING: The Volunteer's Molester

Also a female, aged 12. Erinna, the cross-eyed daughter of a sponge diver registered as Hymenaeus; and an allegedly dead mother. Scheduled, as of Mounichion 6, to die in the Volunteer's stead, barring the unlikelihood of the Volunteer's publicly pardoning her on the morning of the sacrifice, immediately preceding the traditional wedding walk to the city gates. —

The hour having reached 10:50 in the morning, and not having been summoned by my Charge, who had summoned me at daybreak during the 351 preceding days spent in my care, I took the initiative to enter the Municipal Bridal Chamber, where I found my Charge still asleep on her bed. But looking grey. The breath was slow and labored. The skin felt cold to the touch.

As I have been taught by observation and practice, and by preceding oral instructions received mainly from my mother, the healing woman and midwife Kalimera, in preparation for my position as Municipal Attendant to Thargelia Volunteers, and other sacrificial bodies, either purchased or recruited, and kept for emergency calamities, I lifted my Charge from her bed and turned her upside down, making the body stand on the head to reverse the flow of blood and induce vomiting in case the body had been poisoned. Soon a dark brownish fluid started oozing from the lips, although she neither came to nor awakened. I therefore placed the body back on the bed and wrapped it in hot linen, while massaging the region of the heart with fresh nettles.

After a while to my satisfaction the body began to respond to my treatment. The breath came stronger, and more regular. The eyes opened, and eventually she recognized me. She is now resting comfortably, and will be able to undergo the sacrifice as initially scheduled.

As to my additional Charge, my (first) Charge's cross-eyed 12-year-old Molester, scheduled to be stoned to death in the place of my (first) Charge, barring the unlikelihood of my (first) Charge's granting her a public pardon, I am forced to report the girl's disappearance. She was not in the room when I entered at 10:50 this morning. When I found a large sponge of high quality lying in the place of her head on the cot on which she had been allowed to sleep. (Sponge attached to Record.) I hope that the Molester's disappearance will not appear as negligence on my hitherto flawless record.

Considering: That, when I first caught the cross-eyed girl, after she threw a stone at my (first) Charge on Mounichion 6 —as per my Report of Mounichion 6—

I prepared to keep her chained to the wall of the Municipal Bridal Chamber by her ankles, on the ankle hooks provided for that purpose. But my (first) Charge wished that her Molester be allowed to move freely about the room, share her meals, her walks, and most other privileges traditionally accorded Volunteers only. I had no choice but to acquiesce, my first and foremost duty as Official Municipal Attendant being to fulfill all reasonable requests of Thargelia Volunteers, short of providing them with means of escape, which Volunteers in my care and experience have never requested.

My (first) Charge took compassionate interest in her Molester, because of the Molester's age and underprivileged (nurseless) upbringing as a sponge diver's child, without the benefit even of a mother. She drew a chart on the Municipal Wall of the Chamber, above the ankle hooks, to correct the crossing of the Molester's left eye. And she taught the Molester to read, and even to write. Convincing me that the Molester was kept safe, though moving freely about, in the room and on walks, under her and my two-fold vigilance.

This was before my (first) Charge showed an equally compassionate interest in the Molester's father, the sponge diver Hymenaeus, from whom she ordered 3 large sponges for her Municipal Baths, on Mounichion 19. Which the City purchased, as per my Report of Mounichion 19. They are sponges of high quality and should remain usable in my care for several years of Thargelia Volunteers.

By Mounichion 21, the sponge diver Hymenaeus had ensnared my (first) Charge, with the devious cunning that is second nature to persons of his profession, and was going in and out of the Municipal Building at all hours of day and night. —As per my Report of Mounichion 21.

As stated in said Report:

I was not in a position to prevent the increasingly frequent visits of the sponge diver Hymenaeus since they were occurring at my (first) Charge's request, and were giving her visible satisfaction.

Denying the sponge diver Hymenaeus access to the Municipal Building would have violated my first and foremost Duty as Attendant to Thargelia Volunteers. Which is:

To fulfill all reasonable requests, short of providing my Charges with means of escape. Although I instantly suspected that the sponge diver Hymenaeus' exaggerated demonstrations of passion toward my (first) Charge, in the presence of his daughter, and often also in my presence, had the devious purpose of obstructing Municipal Justice, for the benefit of his daughter.

I increased my vigilance, never left the Molester unwatched, either by me or by my (first) Charge. When she sent me out on errands when the Molester's father came to visit her, I always made sure I took the Molester along.

I was present also yesterday, Thargelion 3, during the

entire afternoon, while my (first) Charge sat in the Municipal Patio with the Molester and the Molester's father, drinking new wine. Of which the Molester's father offered, from his own cup, also to the Molester. Who accepted, but instantly spat out what she had sipped. He then urged my (first) Charge to offer wine also to me, but from her cup. Naturally I refused.

I have since then found traces of Hemlock in one of the two cups I provided. But I did not, at any time, upon my Attendant's honor and hitherto flawless Record, see anything being added to the wine in either cup. Even though I never turned my back and carefully observed each frequent refilling of both cups.

The sponge diver Hymenaeus appeared to be quite drunk when he left, before I served my Charges their supper. And he appeared to be considerably drunker when he reappeared at 3 a.m., carrying the large sponge of high quality which I found on the Molester's cot this morning. And turned in as evidence to be attached to the present Record.

In view of the above I beg the Municipal Authorities not to charge my Record with Negligence. Of which I plead innocent, in all honesty. But to consider me sufficiently punished by the premature loss   in 2 days, on Thargelion 6 of my (first) Charge. The only Charge in my experience who is neither deformed nor diseased, not destitute, nor otherwise repulsive. But a normal woman. Even of undeniable attractiveness, although she spends much of her waking time on unwomanly occupations, such as the writing and reciting of poetry.

Who, without the unlawful removal of her Molester, would have remained in my care for the extra year

granted her by the City Fathers. (An extra-long intercalary year of 384 days.)

IMPRINT OF THE RIGHT PALM of
Lithozelos
Municipal Attendant to Thargelia
Volunteers
SIGNED: Lykaios
Maker and Keeper of Municipal Records

Erinna: an Athenian poetess (around 275 BC), who died at
the age of 19.

Thargelion 6

2 more hours until dawn.

Why did my lover not steal me also? I cry to Circe inside
my head. He has a well-trained body, used to defying
steeper challenges than scaling down a municipal wall with
a 30-year-old poetess holding on to his back. During the
darkest hour before dawn, when the City of Athens buries
her dead.

He has perfect night vision, just like a fish.

I would have made myself as light as a sponge: I say to
Circe. Which is what my lover used to say to me: That I
felt as light as a sponge, when he'd lift me off my feet. &
whirl about the room with me, holding me high above his
head. Marvelling at the lightness of my body, despite the
fullness of my breasts. Praising my waist, which he could

span with his hands. My narrow wrists, my ankles. My
slender elongated thighs & legs.

Which I felt glad to have, for his sake. Grateful to & for
my body, for the first time in my life. But which angers
me now. Because it wasn't good enough not to be left
behind. Because it lost out to the scrawny body of a
cross-eyed adolescent girl, who had just bled herself into
womanhood. I might as well be a stone too heavy to lift.
Which is how my heart feels in my abandoned useless
breast.

Why—why—WHY! I cry to Circe.

Because the legitimate relationship always wins out in
the end: she says in an oily drawl. Odysseus had been
blissful with her on her island, but in the end he left her
—& other women before & after her— to return to his
lawful weaving wife. Who dropped her 50 suitors to take
back her lawful philandering husband.

But that was different. My lover is not married to Erinna.
He is Erinna's father! *I*'d never won out over any of *my*
father's lovers! Except for his one brief summer gesture.
Which he denied he'd made as soon as my mother nagged
him about it. Making me think that I had perhaps imagined
it all.

Perhaps I *had* imagined it all: Circe says, oily-voiced.
At least the implications of it. The promise I'd imagined
hearing in my father's whisper.

Why had I made my father the center of my adolescent
fantasies? she asks. Betraying my sex & the moon
wanting to be my mother's rival, rather than her ally.
Had I hoped that my father would take me to bed?

No! I shout, outraged. Never! All I wanted was his
attention. To be made to feel that I existed, by being
acknowledged. I wasn't asking for any spectacular
demonstrations, like being rescued piggy-back down a

municipal wall at dawn, at the expense of any of my father's lovers.

I would have been just as content to have my mother's attention. But my mother was lost to me in her endless conjugal dinner recriminations. Whereas my father . . .

Whereas my father had won every dinner battle I'd sat in on: Circe laughs, sounding ugly in my head. I had coveted the winner: she laughs. Obviously I'd been in love with authority, like most adolescents.

But I hate hate hate HATE authority! I shout, outraged. & perplexed.

Now I do: Circe says. After I felt rejected by authority, during my 12th to 13th summer. Which was fortunate for the joint cause of women & the moon. Whose plight I might never have noticed if I'd felt loved by authority. The way Erinna feels loved by her father. People rarely question an authority that coddles them: Circe laughs her ugly laugh.

Erinna *is* loved by her father! I cry hotly. More than I was loved by her father. *Or* by mine.

& he needn't have stolen her. I was going to forgive her anyway.

Well, now I won't have to. I've been relieved of the choice I've been complaining about for the last 29 days. Ever since Erinna threw the choice in my face. Now I can once again concentrate on our worthy cause: To lead greed to its death, & put an end to the self-righteous raping of all that is life-giving on this earth. Including the earth herself. Not to mention the moon. Now I can concentrate on reestablishing the social balance between men & women, & stay the annihilation of the universe with my sacrifice.

Which I will not feel, as long as I keep chewing the laurel leaves she providentially procured for me.

Which are illegal, incidentally, & may be made available only to Pythian priestesses.

Which I appreciate.

Although I fail to understand why an immortal goddess of the Moon, Circe, the reputed extractor & dispenser of drugs suddenly bothers with man-made laws. Surely such restrictions apply strictly to mortals. & even to mortals such laws mean merely that the drug is harder to get, & more expensive. Entailing unpleasant consequences if the user gets caught in the act. Does Circe think I'm not grateful enough for her softening the ordeal she convinced me to bring upon myself.

For causes that concerned me only as fillers for my audienceless, loveless life.

& are doomed. By the same laws that restrict the use of consciousness-altering drugs, for the purpose of preserving the individual for the conscious experience of total annihilation.

The sole tangible result of my sacrifice will be my parents' embarrassment. Whether they barricade themselves in their house, or feel compelled to come out & watch their shame instead of relying on reports about it from their slaves.

Which gives me no sense of triumph. Doing what embarrasses my parents no longer motivates me. Even if I'll be embarrassing them much more today than all the years I lived my willfully isolated boarder's life under their roof, writing private poems. I freed myself from my parents when I walked out on them 353 days & 9 hours ago.

I walked out at 8 p.m. on Thargelion 6 of last year. It is now 1 more hour until the dawning of my doom's day.

It is thanks to her if I freed myself from my parents: Circe says. Don't I feel that she gave meaning to my life when she gave me something to die for. Or would I rather have continued to live as before. Until I buried my less embarrassed parents. When their house would be taken from me, if it's true what I told her: That women in Athens are no longer allowed to own property. Unless I found someone to marry me. Which would become less & less likely, at 40, at 45, at 50. When I would join the ranks of the roofless poor. A petrified virgin who would eventually die of old age or sickness or anonymity. An old audience-less poetess, of whose passing no one in Athens would take notice.

Surely I was better off incurring the gratitude of future generations of women not to mention of the Moon by a sacrifice I will barely feel after all the laurel leaves I've been chewing.

The illegality of which she mentioned merely to warn me to stop chewing in front of my attendant. Whose municipal servant's conscientiousness might compell him to confiscate what I have left, if he continues to see me shoving leaves into my mouth by the handful.

Which is what I've been doing, since my superfluous awakening yesterday morning. After the realization that I'd been left behind by my daughter-thief of a lover.

Whom Circe also providentially procured for me. Which was not illegal. Merely socially unacceptable. & is costing me the relatively painless death my mother had initially promised me, in the dignified privacy of my municipal chamber.

Which my conscientious attendant would have prevented, if he had caught me at it: Circe says sternly. & rightfully so. It would have been a total waste of death. A death that would have served neither my continued love life, nor future women, nor the moon. Besides condemning an innocent 12-year-old, whom I was totally forgetting, & wouldn't have been able to forgive if I'd committed suicide.

Adding Erinna's death to my own. Gratuitously, without any redeeming cause. Except for the traditional aches & ills of my stone-throwing fellow Athenians. Which was probably what my lover had suspected when he stole his daughter.

But I didn't have any hemlock. My mother hadn't brought me any, after she felt humiliated by my providentially provided sponge diver lover. As an extension of my father's alleged humiliation.

& why hadn't my lover stolen me also, while he was at it. Erinna could easily have scaled down the municipal wall on her own. After she watched her father do it. With me clinging to his back. She imitates everything else her father does. Or says.

Except for loving me. Which she only pretended to do, to save her life.

Also in imitation of her father, perhaps. Whose love for me had perhaps never lost sight of his ulterior motive.

Which my mother had understood instantly. From my father's description of my lover, before she came to visit. Which is why she came to visit without bringing me the promised hemlock.

My lover's ulterior motive had never dissolved into the genuine lust, grateful flesh, & subsequent love *I* had felt. I alone had been stupid enough or perhaps arrogant enough to feel loved, & love back.

Loving isn't stupid: Circe says, in an admonishing schoolteacher's tone. Although I'd certainly been arrogant, in the exuberance of my satisfied flesh. Mercilessly teasing the patient sponge diver. Torturing him with my mock indecision: Who shall it be? Your daughter . . . Your lover? Your lover . . . Your daughter? Who shall live & who shall die?

What proof of love had I expected from the poor man?

Whose motivations were as muddled & multiple as those
of most mortals.

His lust for me had been genuine enough. As surely I
must have noticed. Why couldn't I be satisfied with that.
Would I rather go to my death without having had the
experience of fulfilled desire.

I must have known from the start that my involvement
with a sponge diver would have no future. Surely I don't
seriously envision myself as a sponge diver's wife. Or
concubine. Mothering the motherless Erinna who
increasingly taxes my patience on some cowflap of an
island far from Athens.

Where an immortal goddess might enjoy living, ser-
enely, if it weren't for her fear for the Moon. But not an
audienceless poetess, a 30-year-old mortal who craves
an audience to applaud her vociferous affirmations of
independence.

Do I really see myself bleaching sponges, which salt-
cures the white softness of my hands, used only to writing.
Preparing frugal sponge divers' meals, consisting of: 1
daily bran bun, 1 onion, sow thistles, & a handful of
mushrooms. & perhaps an occasional fish my lover-hus-
band or my step-daughter encounter on their diving
expeditions. For sponges they cannot sell on the island
which is too small to have commerce.

Where I live uncomfortably, feeling out of place, con-
spicuously vertical between the sky & the ocean. With no
time to write my poems. Which Erinna is writing in my
place, while I bear sponge-diving children. To a less & less
loving man who cannot earn the scanty living he eked out
in the city. Where he eventually returns without me,
modeling himself after his hero Ulysses.

Leaving me to raise my sponge-diving sons. To avenge
their father's desertion.

& eventually one of my sons sets out, & finds the
unsuspecting sponge diver, his father, still diving for
sponges, & selling them, & still attractive to women. &
kills him for me.

Just as Telegonus, one of Circe's sons with Odysseus,
eventually sailed to Ithaca. & found Odysseus, still brag-
ging, & bending bows no other man could bend, & still
attractive to women, & killed him.

With an arrowhead fashioned from the bone of a fish.
His aim guided by the sea god Poseidon, whose son, the
cyclops Polyphemus, was being avenged at the same time,
because Odysseus had blinded Polyphemus. & afterwards
mocked him.

& I'll start composing poems of revenge. After I've
grown too old to do anything else. Anything useful biolog-
ically. & have perhaps also grown blind, like Homer.

Whose Odyssey had, incidentally, been written by the
virgin Princess Nausicaa, who'd found Odysseus naked in
the bullrushes on the shore of Scheria & had taken him
home to her father's palace. & whose original tale was
much edited & rewritten, to make Odysseus appear more
heroic, & the women he courted &/or betrayed & kept
waiting more submissive. & the knowledgeable healer &
moon goddess Circe who had offered him refuge on her
island into an evil castrating seductress who changed men
into pigs.

& all this lying & avenging will breed more lies &
murders. & keep pain alive, while all else dies on this
earth. & the moon falls from the sky. Is that what I want!

I shrug. Even if I did want it exile-frugality-discomfort-
motherhood-abandonment after my successful escape, I

cannot have it. Not any more than I can have my mother's mercifully offered/mercilessly withheld hemlock.

I'm lying on my bed which feels immense, without the confines of my lover's arms in my municipal bridal chamber which feels ominously quiet without the sounds of Erinna's breathing.

—Who was not as innocent as Circe would have her be. Who was after all a Thargelia volunteer molester. —

I'm chewing laurel leaves by the fistful, watching the sky grow light over this last morning of my life.

My mouth feels thick, exhausted from uninterrupted chewing. Rule us, Moonliar: I say with lazy tongue & lips.

Circe inside me vaguely wonders if she should take offense. But then decides to humor me. Saying that I should indeed let her rule me, for the duration of the sacrifice. That she'll take over. Casting a full-moon glow about my body that will shroud me in ecstasy, an anæsthetic more powerful than any drug.

Rule us Moonliar is an anagram of the name of the author.